Praise for *See No Color*

"Baseball. Family secrets. First love. Hard truths. *See No Color* hits all this and more. Gibney presents a smooth-flowing narrative, complicated questions, and a powerful protagonist who finds her own real answers."

Pat Schmatz, author of *Bluefish*

"*See No Color* by Shannon Gibney is a groundbreaking coming-of-age story whose appealing heroine, Alex, will have you rooting for her from the beginning. Alex's previously (mostly) coherent sense of identity and family begins to crack, shift, and open up as she explores various secrets and silences, most importantly the silences that have been growing within her. Alex, in fits and starts, begins to take charge of who she is, which is thrilling to witness. The deftly drawn trials and tender triumphs of this black biracial adoptee will resonate with all readers."

Sun Yung Shin, poet and co-editor of
Outsiders Within: Writing on Transracial Adoption

"In *See No Color*, Shannon Gibney makes plain through her protagonist Alex's story that being both black and adopted is complicated. Gibney honestly portrays hardships that black adoptees may face, such as racist comments from family members and the awkwardness of encountering other black people. As the story unfolds, Alex comes to a better understanding of being an adopted black teenager in a white world, but the journey is not easy, nor is it over by the book's end. Drawing on Gibney's own experiences as a transracial adoptee, *See No Color* is a powerful and necessary story."

Sarah Park Dahlen, Assistant Professor of Library Science and
co-editor of *Diversity in Youth Literature:
Opening Doors Through Reading*

SEE NO
Color

SHANNON GIBNEY

HOLIDAY HOUSE · NEW YORK

Text copyright © 2015 by Shannon Gibney
HOLIDAY HOUSE is registered in the U.S. Patent and Trademark Office.
Printed and bound in April 2020 at Maple Press, York, PA, USA.
www.holidayhouse.com
1 3 5 7 9 10 8 6 4 2

All editions are published by arrangement with Carolrhoda Lab,
a division of Lerner Publishing Group, Inc., 241 First Avenue North,
Minneapolis, MN 55401 U.S.A.

Library of Congress Cataloging-in-Publication Data
Gibney, Shannon.
See no color / by Shannon Gibney.
pages cm
Summary: Alex has always identified herself as a baseball player,
the daughter of a winning coach, but when she realizes that is not enough
she begins to come to terms with her adoption and her race.
ISBN 978-1-4677-7682-0 (lb : alk. paper) —
ISBN 978-1-4677-8814-4 (eb pdf)
[1. Identity—Fiction. 2. Baseball—Fiction. 3. Adoption—Fiction.
4. African Americans—Fiction. 5. Self-acceptance—Fiction.
6. Family life—Fiction.] I. Title.
PZ7.1.G5See 2015
[Fic]—dc23   015001619

ISBN 978-0-8234-4568-4 (paperback)

For the others

"That was the miscast summer of my barren youth which (for that short time, that short brief unreturning springtime of the female heart) I lived out not as a woman, a girl, but rather as the man which I perhaps should have been."

—William Faulkner, *Absalom, Absalom!*

PROLOGUE

I am six, safe on his lap. A scorecard on the table, pencil falling out of my hand. *Write the names of your teammates here*, he says, moving my hand slowly left to right, *A*s and *N*s and *E*s smushed together slowly into words. Like magic. *One page for your team, one page for the other.* I nod, because I know what he wants. Not because I am listening right. *You record what happens at each at bat on your scorecard.* He scratches my head, how I like it. *Little Kirtridge.* I laugh. He makes a line from the circle past the square and asks me why he did that. I don't know. I don't know. But he needs some words from me. Now. *That's what happens*, I say. *That's what you put down.* He laughs, even though that is not all the way it works. I want to color in the circle and square, but more I want words from him. So, I put my head on his shoulder, while more words come, and he moves my pencil all around the paper. *You have to keep score in order to win*, he says. *That is what all this adds up to, see?* I close my eyes, and the dreams are almost coming now, with the words. His arms, all blankets, warm me.

PART
One

CHAPTER
ONE

"Go tell Dad we got to get going," Jason commanded. He might have been only a year younger, but these days, he wasn't trying to act like it. I didn't like taking orders from my little brother but decided to leave it alone. I figured he had his hands full trying to negotiate Dad's disappointment, and avoidance was his newest strategy.

Like me, Jason would do anything to avoid *the look*—the stern and disapproving glance Dad gave us whenever we had done wrong in the game. *When you don't play your best, you don't just hurt yourself. You hurt me.* His eyebrows would knit together, his lips even tighter than usual and he would emit this kind of energy from his eyes that could scald. I knew that Jason didn't want to see last week's game and his lackluster performance reflected in Dad's eyes.

I shrugged and stared into my copy of *The Scarlet Letter*. "We've still got two hours before first pitch." West High, which Dad had been coaching for seven years, was hoping to make it to the state tournament.

Jason glared at me, pressing his right arm into the wall. "Alex, you know how he gets when he doesn't have enough time to do the whole warm-up."

I remembered the game last year when I couldn't find a tampon or pad in the entire house and we had to stop at Walgreen's. We still got to the game very early, but Dad's face was pinched for the next day and half. He was so irritated with me. And plus, my game was just *off* for seven long innings. No, Jason was right—I definitely didn't want to go through that again, especially before such an important game. If I had to do my homework reading later tonight and postpone *The Walking Dead* graphic novels I'd set aside as a reward, then so be it. I stood up, reluctantly, and then pushed in my chair. "Where is he?"

Jason turned around and began stretching his other arm. "He's down in the den, messing around with some of his files or something."

I rolled my eyes and started walking down the long, French-tiled hallway. Dad spent hours in that den, doing God knows what. Poring over various files, reading all his special baseball analytics newsletters, watching, cutting, and reordering video clips of our games, and most of all, checking and adding to his ever-growing battery of stats and metrics. Walking in there was like walking inside his brain; it was too intense and almost creepy.

I rounded the corner and started down the steps to the den. The cool stone against my bare feet sent shivers up my spine, and my hands grabbed my elbows. A full color print-out of last season's metrics for both Jason and me was plastered across the right-side wall, lest either of us—or worse, Dad—committed the deadly sin of forgetting. I read the slash lines again, involuntarily:

ALEX: .311/.403/.561

JASON: .287/.377/.539

Batting average/on-base percentage/slugging percentage—three numbers that managed to be us. When I looked up, I spotted Dad, leaning over his big, gray filing cabinet, rifling through its folders. His brow was furrowed in concentration as he lifted one of them up and paged through its contents slowly and methodically. I leaned against the wall, still not in plain sight, but not really hidden either. I was relieved for some reason that he hadn't noticed me, even though I had come here to get his attention, to tell him that we needed to go.

He pulled out an envelope that looked very worn and tattered and quite old. He ran his fingers over it gently, like he was reading braille. I don't think I had ever seen my father handle something so carefully, and I wondered what it was. He bit his lip and then sighed. After a moment, he pulled out a letter and opened it slowly, smoothing out the folds. He was holding it at such an angle that I could not read it, but I could have made out the handwriting if I recognized it. I craned my neck out, curiosity trumping fear.

"Time to go?" His head had snapped around so quickly that I was hearing the words before seeing his eyes.

I jumped. "Yes!" I said, too brightly. "It's twelve thirty." I shoved my hands into my pockets.

He smiled, crammed the letter and envelope back into the folder, and slammed the cabinet closed. I jumped again at the sound.

"Sorry, honey," Dad said, walking briskly to his chair to get his coat. "Just got caught up." His shoulders looked a little tight, but the rest of his body looked loose, so I hoped I was off the hook. He didn't seem angry.

He strode over to me and put his arm around my shoulder. "Shall we?"

I nodded, willing myself to lean into him, to make his embrace comfortable. Then we began to walk back toward the kitchen, in a kind of awkward silence. I wanted to ask him so many things. But before I could even fathom opening my mouth, we were in the kitchen, facing Jason, who was sprawled out on the floor in the runner's stretch. "Time to go out and get a win," Dad said, clapping his hands. Jason's shoulders hunched, and he kind of shivered in surprise at the sharpness of the sound, almost like Dad was waking him up or something. He looked up at him and nodded grimly.

CHAPTER
TWO

It was a cool late March day, with just a little bit of dew on the ground, and green just beginning to push through the hard soil. A few family and friends dotted the bleachers surrounding the field, arranging their coolers and jackets and seat-rests. I closed my eyes and inhaled deeply, trying to take it all in, and prepare myself for the first step toward winning the state tournament and, at the same time, a place on the elite club team this summer and fall. When I opened my eyes, I saw Dad walking out to meet the other coach on the pitcher's mound. The game was against East, our crosstown rivals. The rest of us gathered as close as we dared, throwing and catching and warming up, but really just trying to listen. Dad was famous for trying to get in the heads of his rival managers.

"John," Dad said, thrusting his hand toward the wide, lumbering man who approached him wearing a cockeyed East High cap and sweatpants that were a little too big. "So good to see you," said Dad. "How are Katie and the kids?" He and Dad had gone to Clemson together. Dad had broken every record while he was there, while this other guy had been more of a fixture on the bench.

The man smiled warmly, and grasped Dad's hand. "They're great, Terry. Great. And Rachel and the kids?"

"Good, good. Everyone's good." Dad paused, looking down into the other team's dugout. Lots of pale, skinny Wisconsin kids. Not much power. "Looks like you got a promising bunch this year. We're ready for a first-rate outing today," said Dad.

The man beamed, then slapped Dad on the back. Both of them laughed and then stared up at the sky. I got the feeling that they really didn't have that much more to say to each other, but they had to wait for the umpire to meet them up there to begin.

"Been hearing about this center fielder you got. A girl, I hear— a black girl. Heard she's got some legs on her, that she can hit, too."

"That's Alex," Dad said, crossing his arms over his chest. "My daughter."

The man had tiny, beady eyes, but they fluttered open. He brought his left hand to his neck and began to rub it. You could almost hear the thoughts running through his head: *black daughter, white father, white mother, white brothe*r . . .

"You adopted," the man said, finally getting it. "You and Rachel." He squinted into the sunlight. "I'm sure you told me before, and I just forgot." The umpire was finally making his way toward them. I thanked God because all the warm-up chatter had died and no one was even throwing anymore. I could feel the tension collecting under my shoulder blades, the hiccups forming in my windpipe.

"She *is* a great player," Dad said. "Phenomenal for a girl, really."

"That so?" asked the man.

Dad shifted his weight and nodded. "She's mixed, not black. She's half white."

The man nodded, and the umpire approached them about beginning the game. I exhaled as the subject changed to defining the exact location of the strike zone, how many umpires were on the field for the day, and where they would be standing.

...

I led off the bottom of the fifth. Since I had an on-base percentage of .403 so far this season, any inning where I was up first had possibilities. I never had power, but I could always get on base since I could hit into the holes and had speed.

We were up, three to two. They had this black pitcher who was supposed to really be something. Apparently, he had just moved to Madison a few months before. He had perfect location in the strike zone and could throw a changeup that would leave you cross-eyed as the ump called you out.

"Look for the fastball and try to adjust to anything off-speed," Dad told me before the game. "And try to pull it to left."

The light spring breeze felt a little too cold on my cheeks, and the sun was already too bright for my sunglasses. I lifted my bat up over my shoulder and planted my feet solidly into the ground. I knew that the pitcher had looked at the scouting report on me, too: .311/.403/.561. You didn't get good without knowing exactly what you were up against. He brought his left hand out of the glove and went into the windup. I knew it would be a high fastball—the pitch that always looks good to hitters but rarely is. He was counting on me to swing, to give into temptation, like Jason had at the end of the last inning when he had struck out. It was coming at me, fast and hard, but I knew it was too high, so I took it. The umpire called a ball.

Out of the corner of my eye, I saw the pitcher flinch. I could hear Dad's voice in my ear: *There's no preparation like over-preparation. Remember, every second, how lucky you are to be playing the game. Appreciate it—really feel it. Because you never know when it could all be taken away from you.* I stepped back into the box. The pitcher was shaking his head at the catcher. Shaking again; they must not be on the same page. I had seen his team.

Finally, they agreed on something. He stretched and delivered. Right up the middle. He wanted that strike, no matter what. I brought the bat around fast and connected. There was a whack, and it flew over the pitcher's head. I pumped my arms, dragged my legs toward first. *Come on, Kirtridge, come on.* Why was first always so incredibly far away? It blurred ahead of me while dust flew up and curled under my cleats. *Come on, come on.* I knew the ball had dropped in the infield, near the shortstop. I brought my foot down on the bag and ran through. My lungs tightened, constricted even though they wanted more air. The umpire stretched his arms out to either side. I exhaled. It was then that I saw the shortstop still holding the ball. I laughed. He hadn't even tried to make the play. The pitcher lifted up his glove, motioning for the shortstop to throw him the ball. You could see he was angry from the way he moved: exaggerated and agitated. I had done my job.

I touched the base and then took a reasonable lead as my teammate stepped up to the plate. The black kid on the mound looked back at me once, over his glove, but I was confident that he wouldn't try to pick me off. He knew exactly how fast I was now. Today, anyway, I was stronger than he was.

CHAPTER
THREE

After we beat East, we went out to dinner with them. This was a league tradition, and when we won, it was a tradition my father loved. In his postgame glee, Dad insisted on paying for everyone. "To my old friend, John," he said, raising a mug of Heineken. "A great coach and a great friend."

You could see that John really didn't want to raise his mug to meet Dad's, that what he really wanted to do was get out of that pizzeria. However, he managed to stick a fake smile on his face and clink his glass with Dad's.

Dad put his arm around John's shoulders and squeezed hard. "This team of yours is really something, John. Really something." Dad rarely, if ever, got drunk in public, but he often got happy. He raised his glass again. "A toast. To the team."

John's face became clouded, but he made the toast. The rest of his team followed with their Cokes and Sprites.

Jason and I exchanged glances across the table; I covered my mouth with my hand and hoped no one could hear me laugh. "He's so crazy," I said in a low voice. You couldn't blame him for being excited, though—we were one step closer to the state tournament.

Jason shook his head. "Man," he said, stirring the ice in his glass with his straw. "I played so bad today."

In truth he had. 1 for 5, 2 SOs, 0 BoBs, 1 E, 0 R. I leaned toward him. "Look, all you have to do is adjust your stance a bit. Keep your shoulder in longer. You're bailing out." Dad would have this all on film and would no doubt make Jason watch all his at bats in slow motion high def tomorrow in the den.

Jason drummed his fingers on the table, eyes drooping. His closely-cropped blond hair barely covered up a welt on his head that he had gotten from a badly played grounder a few games ago. "Don't you ever wonder if this is what you're supposed to be doing?"

I stared at him: his perfectly ironed jersey, his big ears. "What do you mean?"

"I mean the game. At this level, all the time." He threw up his hands. "Alex, you're sixteen, I'm fifteen, and we practice three or four hours a day. Crazy."

I couldn't believe what he was saying. "That's what it takes to be the best, Jason." I put my hand over his, stopping his drumming. I leaned toward him and whispered, "And we are the best. Maybe not right now. Everyone has slumps. You'll pull out of it. The numbers will turn around."

He drew his hand away and shook his head. "I'm sick of being a slash line. I don't love it like you do," he said. His gray eyes looked away from me.

We ran four miles a day at five thirty every morning and lifted weights in the basement when we got home from school. Since I was a girl, Dad said I had to work twice as hard to develop strength, so I lifted ten pounds more than Jason and at more reps. Practice was an hour and a half after weight lifting and usually lasted for two hours, four days a week. I knew what Jason meant about the intensity; I could see he was tired of thinking about it every day. But I didn't believe he didn't love it. That was impossible.

"He would kill me if I told him I wasn't sure about it," he said.

"Shut up. You're sure."

"It's my whole life."

"That's why you'll work harder, get better," I said, sipping my Coke.

He sat up, took a deep breath. Dad was still at the center of the table, lecturing a couple of our teammates—always looking to the next game. "Sometimes I hate him for that," Jason said quietly. Then he stood up and walked to the bathroom. I turned to watch his tall, skinny back recede into the dim lighting of the pizzeria.

"How you doing?" someone asked me from behind. I turned around to see the black pitcher. *He has a good face—high cheekbones and deeply set eyes.* My stomach flipped. He stuck out his hand. "Reggie Carter."

I grabbed his hand and shook it vigorously. "Alex," I said.

He gestured toward the chair across from me. "Mind if I sit down?"

I shook my head. "No, please do." I wondered how long Jason would be in the bathroom.

The pitcher looked over me slowly, and my stomach flipped again. "Girl, you know how to play some ball. How long you been playing with the guys?"

"Always," I said, trying to keep my voice even. *A black guy wants to talk to me.*

He raised his eyebrows. "Always as in . . . Always?"

I laughed nervously. "Yeah. I know that's crazy, but, you know, my dad started me early." *But I'm not really black.*

"Your dad."

I gestured toward Dad, who had finally sat down at a table overflowing with beer and pizza. "My dad."

Reggie looked from Dad to me and back again a few times. "Your . . . oh. Your dad! Terry Kirtridge, right? Oh yeah, I think I can see it." He leaned toward me, examining my face carefully. "Yeah, ya'll got the same pretty eyes, and the same killer swing."

When he smiled, a dimple appeared to the right of his mouth. I shut my eyes as my face started to heat up. I could see the black kids at West High, clustering at all the entryways, looking and laughing at me. There was no way through.

"So your mom then," he was saying. "She's black."

I laughed. "No. She's . . . I mean . . ." He was giving me his full attention. I glanced toward the bathroom; no sign of Jason. "That's right," I told him.

"Wow," he said, looking at Dad again. "That's cool."

I laughed nervously. I had been enjoying his proximity, but now I wished he would just leave. My pulse felt like it was speeding up every second.

"You know, I think it's cool they let you play with the boys and all," he said. "Because I'm sure you would whip some ass in softball." He grinned. "Bet them girls don't like you too much, do they?"

I cringed. "What do you mean?" I fiddled with my unruly hair, which had been in a ponytail as it was for every game, but I was pretty sure that it was frizzing wildly by now.

"Well, you know," he said. "Folks don't usually like people who show them up."

"I guess so," I said. "I don't really have too many girlfriends." Jason rounded the corner, out of the bathroom, fiddling with his fly. In a few strides, he would be beside us. I stood up, rattling the table and almost knocking over my Coke. Reggie caught it before it spilled.

"I've got to use the bathroom," I said. I started walking away from him. "I'll be right back." *He will never talk to you again.*

"Sure," he said. I felt his eyes on my back as I almost ran away.

I stayed in there for almost fifteen minutes, standing on the toilet seat with the door locked. When I finally came out, Reggie and Jason were engaged in a lively conversation—something about East High versus West High parties. I snuck over to the other side of the room and absently pushed the buttons of the pinball machine. Its lights flashed as the metal ball sped and careened

14

off the walls. I wished I could get inside the machine, underneath the glass, and hide. I looked down at the burnt brown skin on my hands, arms, and legs, and wondered how it had come to cover me, how it *was* me.

When I turned around, Reggie was staring at me in confusion. He knew I was a liar. I wanted to walk up to him and say that I hadn't wanted to lie to him, tell him why I had done it. But I had no idea what I would say.

CHAPTER FOUR

Dad's favorite place to go running was by Lorraine Creek on a small path through the woods that he had beat out himself through running there over the years. He said that the trees and the water always felt like they were running with him, like they were the only things moving in the twilight of the early morning. I knew just what he meant.

"Creek's high this season," he said, his breath jagged. It was the Monday after our win against East.

I jumped over a sinkhole. "Yeah."

It had snowed a lot that winter and had only recently begun to warm up. The snow went straight into the waterways, filling them with a ferocity that kept on rising.

"Wish I had that much energy," Dad said.

I tried to laugh, but I was so cold that it came out more like a cough. Some mornings, our four-mile, five-thirty run really kicked my ass, and this was one of them. My sweat felt like a wet blanket wound tightly around my whole body, and I wasn't really awake.

Still, it was my favorite part of the day, especially when it was just me and Dad. Jason's shin splints were flaring up again and he had been ordered not to run for at least a month by our doctor. Unlike me, he hated running and was relieved to have an extra hour of sleep. What he hadn't realized yet was the power that came from pushing your body farther than you thought it could go, the mental fortitude it took to push past shaking legs and wheezing lungs. That was the knowledge that Dad and I shared.

Low-hanging branches whipped around us in the pre-dawn air. Dead leaves crunched under our feet.

"It's okay," I told Dad, my feet light and my legs strong against the trail. "You know, conservation of energy. Physics class stuff. Nothing owns energy. You just use it and then pass it on."

Dad laughed, in between labored breaths. He was working hard but the laugh was easy. Natural. Normal.

I laughed and thought for a split second that I could feel within the new step I was taking now, each of the steps I had taken running on this path with Dad years before. It gave me strength and the conviction that I was doing something meaningful and much larger than myself. If I looked closely, I could almost see the step I had taken almost ten years ago, running my very first mile with Dad by my side, egging me on the whole time, even when I told him I thought my lungs were about to burst. He had simply reached over and squeezed my elbow very gently, and said, "It's okay. You're okay."

And sure enough, I was. I remembered that I got control of my breathing and finished just in front of him. And then I was also eleven on this trail, an avalanche of mud in the middle of a rainy October morning completely taking off my shoe, and then a sharp twig just beneath it slicing open the side of my foot in the next step. How I howled! It seemed like Dad didn't even break stride—he just turned around and scooped me up, ran me all the way home and to the emergency room. *Muuuudddddd!* He would scream playfully whenever we would encounter it now and start gesturing like a crazy man. I would just shake my head and pretend to ignore him, until he poked me enough times that I couldn't help it and started laughing.

"This. Damn. Knee," he said, in between huge sucks of air. "I'm already becoming an old man over here. Every day, a new part of me goes to pieces."

"Becoming?" I asked.

He kicked some dirt onto my calf.

"Hey," I said, "Is that the last resort of the elderly—cheating?"

Dad snorted. "No game going on here. We're just training. You can't cheat in training."

I raised an eyebrow. "Aren't you the same coach who's always telling us we can't cut corners in training, 'cause it's *cheating*? Or was that your younger, more dedicated doppelganger?"

Instead of answering, he burst ahead of me without warning and started to sprint along the path. "I'll check in with you when *you're* forty-three and see if you can do this," he said.

I grinned. "Race you to the top of the hill, old man," I told him as the vista of the valley became visible. The small stand of birch trees at the top was bent over by wind, pulling us forward.

"You're on, Little Kirtridge," said Dad, accelerating even faster. That was the name he had given me after my first game, when I had gotten on base twice and thrown two people out. Everyone was saying that I was "Terry Kirtridge, Jr.," and he simply said, "No, she's just Little Kirtridge."

I grinned and pumped my arms as hard as I could. My breath was like a metronome in my chest, and as my feet clawed into the ground, I could almost hear the rush of water behind me, its progress unstoppable.

CHAPTER
FIVE

My little sister Kit leaned over an impossibly delicate-looking papier-mâché sculpture of a butterfly and pulled a paintbrush across its chest in a movement that seemed both calculated and completely spontaneous. The sharp orange of the paint clashed with the deep green landscape on the other side of the windows and made me feel suddenly awake. I was reading in the living room and had the perfect view of her latest project. This was where I liked to sit when she was in the middle of working because I could be on the edge of the activity while at the same time I could see everything if I wanted to.

"What's the other color going to be?" I asked. She had been confining herself to just two colors lately because she said that color was actually "a seduction"—that it could keep you from developing your other skills as an artist if you let it. Apparently, minimizing color composition was challenging her to express her eleven-year-old self through shape, media, use of perspective, and a host of other elements that my extremely practical sixteen-year-old self could not recall.

"You'll see," she said, flashing me a mischievous grin.

I just snickered and returned to my book. You couldn't keep up with her, so why even try?

Out of the corner of my eye, I watched her walk to the sink, wash the paint off of the brush, and begin to mix a new topaz green color onto her palette. It was flat, not shiny, so it brought out the orange's quieter undertones. She began to paint topaz swirls all along the butterfly's torso with such dexterity that I began to get dizzy from watching her. Finally, she stepped back from the butterfly to inspect her work and make any adjustments needed, I assumed. Her long blond hair was flecked with orange, as was her shirt. I remembered that Mom had taken her on a special back-to-school shopping trip to get that blouse. "Just one fancy one, for nice occasions, please," Mom had begged her. It was a light silk and should not have come anywhere near paint of any kind. But then Kit was never one for common sense.

She had grown into a strange girl, my sister. Everyone said that she would be beautiful, and she was, even at eleven, incredibly beautiful, but I could see it transforming into more of a wild, almost feral kind of beauty. Something you had to look hard to see because she didn't want you to see it at all.

"Nice choice," I said, referring to the topaz. "Not what I would have thought of at all."

She cocked her head to the side, frowning. "You think so? I'm not sure."

"Yeah," I said. "I like it."

Kit walked around the butterfly, painting tiny topaz marks here and there. I knew there was some kind of pattern she was following—some kind of internal logic—but I could not see what it was. "What do you like about it?"

I laughed. She was playing with me or something. I picked up *Dreams from My Father* again, ready to resume reading. "Never mind."

There was a long silence as she continued painting, and I

immersed myself in my book. Our dog Paddington came over and lay down by my feet. I patted his head absently.

"You know, I do value your opinion, Alex," Kit said.

I laughed again. "Okay, whatever." Something was obviously going on in her mind, but I had no idea what it was, and I wasn't going to spend any of my own time trying to pry it out of her.

I heard her stomp her foot, and I put down the book again. I had read to Kit when she was younger—both books that I was reading and books she wanted me to read—and eventually I had even taught her to read. In much the same way Dad and I had our thing running by the creek, Kit and I had our reading. When you train as hard as we did, "recovery time" was a big part of the day. And fighting for more time with Xbox wasn't my thing, so walking with Kit a few blocks to the library at least once a week to stock up became our routine. We'd spend hours sitting near each other, me reading and Kit reading, or sometimes me reading aloud and Kit drawing. Or that was how it used to be. She still wanted to know what I was into at a particular moment, and had nodded her approval when I began Obama's memoir, but something wasn't right. Things refused to click into the old, easy rhythm.

"I'm serious," Kit said. She was facing me directly, her big gray eyes full and intense. "I want to be a better sister." She lowered her gaze for a moment. "I know it's not easy for you."

I stared at her.

She looked impatient. "You know what I mean."

I laughed. "No. As usual, Kit, I don't." *Then why is your heart beating faster?* And then, the image of Dad and the envelope came back into my mind.

Kit's face twisted a little bit, like she was looking at me from far, far away—maybe from space or something.

Dad came in then to get a glass of water, effectively stopping our conversation. He groaned when he saw the butterfly on the table. "Kit, you need to clear all of this off. Now. You know you can't work in here."

Kit whipped around to face him. "Well, where am I supposed to work?"

"Clear it off," Dad said, in his *and that's final* voice. "Mom just got home. She's about to start on dinner." He walked into the living room. "I don't want her to see any of this when she comes in."

Kit didn't say anything but just curled her upper lip at me across the room.

Kit and Dad never seemed to understand each other. That was nothing new.

Dad had given Kit a bat the day she turned six. This was a tradition with Dad—we'd all gotten real bats for that birthday. But he went overboard with Kit. I remember him telling Mom that he knew the perfect bat for her. It was a discontinued model, but that didn't matter to him. He had spent weeks hunting it down, vying with buyers on eBay to get the best deal and bring it home to his youngest prodigy-in-the-making. It was an extra-lightweight MAKO XL2, with a legendary sweet spot. Jason and I, ten and eleven that year, were both jealous but tried to play it off. I remember Kit unwrapping it unceremoniously, the shiny silver paper falling to the ground, and Dad leaning forward eagerly in anticipation.

"What is this?" she asked, frowning.

Mom, Jason, and I glanced at each other anxiously.

"Well, it's a *bat*, sweetie," Dad had said, as if he was talking to a dumb animal, like a cow.

Kit met his intense gaze directly. "I know it's a bat. But I don't want a bat."

Dad laughed. "Well, you don't want a bat *now*, but once you learn how to use it . . ."

"*You* want a bat," she said. "You wanted *this* bat. So, have it." Then she delicately lifted it up and presented it to him in both palms.

I was conscious that I was holding my breath. It had never occurred to me, before that moment, that it was possible to say no to my father about anything—but especially about baseball. I could not imagine what was going to happen. But Dad simply cocked his head to the side, the way a dog does when it hears a strange noise, or sees something it can't quite make sense of. He looked down at the bat, then back up again at Kit, then back at the bat. Then he gently pushed the bat back toward Kit's chest. "What are you . . . I got this for you, honey," he said, almost pleadingly. "Especially for you. You have no idea how—"

Kit's resolve seemed to falter for a moment, and I saw a glimmer of fear in her eyes. Clearly, she did not want the bat, but she had also not thought all the way through this confrontation with Dad. He was, after all, the governing force in our family universe, which is why he always got what he wanted.

Before I could think, I heard myself say, "Hey, the bat's here now, so we can always come back and check it out anytime. I want you to open my present. I picked it out for you special."

Mom shot me a look across the table. I had not picked it out for her special; in fact, I had forgotten about her birthday altogether, like I always did, so Mom had picked out a funny picture book about a llama she thought Kit would like. Had I been there, I would have told her that Kit and I had read it and the entire llama series last year, but I was not there. I reached over and handed Kit the poorly wrapped silver package that I had assembled exactly fifteen minutes before. "Go ahead, open it," I said quickly, anticipating another rebuttal from Dad.

Kit grabbed the package and her chance at escape. "Ooo, cool," she said, shaking it back and forth. "I wonder what it could be." She and I laughed, but no one else did. Dad sat back in his chair and crossed his arms, a sour look spreading over his face. But he let it go, miraculously. "I love this book!" Kit exclaimed, ripping off the paper. Then she winked at me conspiratorially.

Dad tried many, many times after that to get her interested in the game. I think he even got her to hit the ball a few times. Still, she made her distaste for it so plain that it was better for everyone if she was not there while we played, trained, or discussed baseball. Which was most of the time. At first, I felt bad, like we were intentionally leaving her out. But then I realized that she really *wanted* to be left alone to do her own thing—that she was really happier that way. But I think that Dad never really forgave her for that first grand rejection. And the fact that she didn't care about that, either, was always stacked up between them, like a big box of broken trophies.

More and more these days, though, it seemed like the broken stuff was between Kit and me too.

CHAPTER
SIX

Shimmery waves and blue air.
Me floating just under the water, only my face up, breathing,
breathing. I can hear me loud in my ears, and it makes me laugh.
Paddington dives into the lake to get the old baseballs that Jason
throws for him. *What a good dog*, Daddy says, ball-jawed boy swim-
ming back. Mom on land, cooking tomatoes and meat and rice.
Baby Kit beside her, digging shells from the ground. They change
colors, crystal-like, with sunlight. She showed me yesterday when I
was helping watch her. Because she is too little to watch herself. We
put one to our ears and it did not say anything, although Mom told
us it would. To us, it only said, *Whoooooosh! Whooosh!*

I want to stay at the lake cottage always, where it is shimmery
and air open everywhere. I know Mom wants to, too. But we always
have to go home at the end of the week. Because school will start
again. And then the lake and cottage will be here alone.

I am trying to blow bubbles from my nose and the sun is pushing the sky down when she shakes my arm. At first I think I am

drowning, like Mom told me to *be careful of*, that someone is dragging me under. It is not too deep here, but I forget that I have feet and legs, too, so I kick and squirm, and water comes into my eyes and nose. I am coughing and also sinking, but then the lady from the cottage next door pulls me up out of the heavy water, both of her arms grabbing my shoulders.

You're boating the mar from your most family, she says, and she is squiggly and kind of melting. I laugh. She frowns. *You're floating too far from your host family*, she says. This time I understand her words. Kind of. I get my legs under me, feet touching sand, brush water from my eyes and she is not squiggly anymore, she is an old lady who is mad. Mad at me?

Your host family, she says again. *You need to get back to them.* I try to smile at her, to make her not mad, but the smile falls out of my mouth too quick. The old lady sticks her face in mine. *Do you speak English? Where are you from? Can you understand me?* She looks like a witch from the Halloween book who has lost her hat, so I laugh again. *I don't know if they swim where you're from, but here, children need to swim close to the shore. It's dangerous. You should be careful.* The laughing stops. There is that word again: *careful*. I was not being *careful*, like Mom said.

I try to back up, toward the shore, away from the lady witch who smells like garlic. Then Mom is beside me, wading into the lake, all towel and top-of-head kisses. *What seems to be the problem?* Looking to Mom to me, no words come from the lady, but she is still speaking with her eyes. *Was my daughter bothering you somehow?* I whip around to Mom's eyes. *No, Mom! I was just floating. Then she grabbed me for no reason.* Then the words crawl out of the space between the lady's lips, spider-like. *She's . . . How is she your daughter?* Mom's face is empty, nothing there at all except her eyes, blinking. *She's your host daughter, then? From Africa?* Mom's eyes explode. *What are you talking about? This is my daughter, Alex. I just wanted to make sure she was all right, since you were—*The light on the waves is shimmering back and forth. *But she's black!* The lady says. She spits it out, *black*, like a bug in her mouth. Black. Black. Black. Black. Black. Black. Black. I say it over and over in my mouth and later that night in my bed. *I am black. Black. Black. Black. Black. Black.* Something else. Something dark, in the night. Dad, Mom, Jason, Kit, are not. *She's adopted*, Mom says, pulling me into her side. *Not that it's any of your business.* She turns us around, and we are walking back to our part of the beach, the waves turning darker. I see my hand now, beside hers, and for the first time it is *brown*. Hers is not, hers is *light. I am brown and they are light*, I whisper to myself. Mom's legs are stiff boards, and she is huffing. *Listen to me, Alex*, she is saying. *That woman doesn't know what she is talking about, okay? She is just . . . crazy.* I move my head up and down, because she wants it. *We are all one in this family, okay? We don't even see color.* I want to ask her what she means, but I know she needs me not to. *Right?* She says. *Right*, I say. I need her hand, so I take it, and Jason and Dad come to us, and they are *light*, and I am *black/brown* as I wiggle my toes deep into the sand. *Adopted*, I whisper to it, remembering the witch lady's words. *That is also what I am.* But I don't understand.

CHAPTER SEVEN

"Katherine, please pass the salt," Mom said at dinner. Half the time I didn't know who she was talking about when she used that name, and I knew I wasn't the only one. Mom had maintained a perverse dislike of Kit's nickname since she was a child and still held out the hope—however slim—that she might someday revert back to the name given to her at birth.

Kit lazily reached for the saltshaker and took her time to hand it to Mom. I knew she hated her formal name as much as Mom loved it.

"I like these cheddar potatoes," Dad said, spooning a second helping onto his plate. "New recipe?"

Mom nodded and then took the saltshaker from Kit. "Got it from *Cooking Light*. It's part of their new summer issue on quick and easy sides." She sprinkled a dash of salt on her green beans as she babbled on. "I saw about a million more recipes for things that would be perfect. Roasted beets, sweet potato fries, fresh cabbage salad. That magazine is a miracle."

Dad shoveled a full forkful of potatoes into his mouth and grunted his agreement.

I felt a laugh bubbling up from the bottom of my stomach and looked across the table to Jason to share in the absurdity of the moment. Were we in the middle of a *Cooking Light* commercial? But he was too busy cutting up his pork chop to notice my glance. Beside him, however, I felt Kit's eyes probing my own. They were huge and filled with mischief. I looked away before I laughed out loud.

"What do you think, Alex?" Mom asked me out of nowhere.

I chewed on a piece of pork chop. Suddenly, all eyes were on me. "What do I think about what?"

Mom stabbed a bean with her fork and began to cut it with her knife. "What do you think of the potatoes?"

"Oh . . . yeah, they're delicious."

Mom smiled, satisfied with my answer. She always needed to have her cooking abilities praised. It was annoying, but necessary. Dad turned to Jason to ask something about school, but I was distracted by Kit. Something was going on. She made a screwed up face at me and I looked away again.

Then Kit clanged her fork onto her plate and folded her fingers together, almost as if in prayer. "What do you all make of Alex being the only black person in our family? I mean, I've been thinking about it, and I know I'm not the only one. Sometimes I see people staring at us in the grocery store like they can't figure us out, and I feel weird, and then I know it must be like ten times weirder for Alex. But it's like this *secret*, you know? Like no one is supposed to actually admit that *she's black*, or maybe more that *she's not white*. But it's impossible because she's just right there, with us and it's like, 'How can't you see this?'" She said it in a completely credulous tone, no different from Mom's rambling on about the recipes.

Mom coughed on her potatoes, and Dad set his wineglass on the table with a thud. I stopped chewing and shoved a long, stray, frizzy curl back into my ponytail.

For a minute, the air was thick with electricity, and then Dad spoke. "Excuse me?"

Kit looked him straight in the face, clear-eyed, and repeated the question. She had never asked anything like that before, but then again, she seemed to grow bolder—and more careless—every day. This must have been what she was trying to address with me earlier. I tried to decide if I was angry or just surprised, and what I realized I was feeling most at that moment was fear. It wasn't what I'd expected.

Dad's jaw was set, and he picked up the wineglass again. "Alex is only half black," he said.

I couldn't even look at him.

He cleared his throat and stared down Kit. "And there are lots of white families who adopt black children, anyway. You know that as well, so I'm not sure what you're getting at." He squinted at Kit. "Is there something going on with you? You're acting even stranger than usual lately."

Jason looked completely perplexed. I could sense him trying to catch my eye, but I was trained on Kit, waiting for her response.

Kit shrugged, nonchalantly meeting Dad's glare. "Lulu says that even though Alex is mixed and dresses like a white kid, people think she's black when they look at her." Lulu was the black girl who lived across the street, and also Kit's best friend. "And she was also asking me why our family adopted Alex when you already had Jason and me."

Mom's face was flaming red, and she was breathing hard. "You hadn't even been born yet when we got Alex, and I had no idea I was going to get pregnant with Jason." The words were spilling out of her, like she didn't know where they were coming from. "And anyway, what business is it of Lulu's? Why would you even be talking about personal family stuff with Lulu anyway? That's not her business! That's nobody's business but ours." She shook her head and blinked at Kit, like she didn't know her.

Kit sighed. "She asked."

I felt *my* face turn red. My clothes felt too tight. So people were talking about me in the neighborhood? *What else are they saying about your not-so-black ass?*

"Lots of people will ask you lots of things," Dad said, holding Kit's eyes with his own. "Things which absolutely do not concern them. And when that happens, it's your job—no, your *responsibility*—not to answer them. Some things are just private."

"And this is not exactly dinnertime conversation," Mom said, her voice wobbly.

I wanted to say something. I wanted to tell them to quit talking about me like I wasn't there, but I didn't know what words to use. And yet, at the same time, there was a part of me that was grateful to Kit for saying something and grateful to Lulu for being able to verbalize what I could not.

Kit laughed. "Alex being black is *private*?"

I looked, alarmed, between Dad and Kit. Not two feet away from her, he looked like he wanted to slap her. But she either didn't see this or didn't care. "I mean, I get how some parts of her *adoption* are private. Or at least that you guys *want* it to be pri—"

Mom grabbed Kit's arm and hissed, "Be *quiet*, young lady!" I swear I could see tears in her eyes.

But it was like Kit was a ghost, outside her body, because she wasn't even fazed, didn't seem to even register that Mom was clutching her. "I mean, what if Alex's other parents can teach her about black people, so maybe she wouldn't feel so—"

"Shut up!" Mom and Dad both yelled at the same time. It was like two cymbals striking with Kit between them.

Kit looked stunned, like she had just woken up, except that the waking world was much worse than her dream.

I clenched my fists tightly under the table. Then I pushed my chair out and ran from the table.

"Alex!" Mom called after me. And in the background I heard, "See what you did?"

When I got to my room, I played Maroon 5 as loud as it would go and dove under my covers. There were times like this when I wanted to just disappear, when my body seemed to be more trouble than it was worth. And the worst part was that I knew that later everyone would act like nothing had happened. That was always just the way it went.

CHAPTER
EIGHT

I am not stupid. I see things. I catch certain repeated phrases. I can sense discomfort. I notice willful blindness. There was, for example, the matter of the video clips Dad dug up on YouTube of Hank Aaron talking about hitting more than twenty home runs for twenty straight seasons. "You'll learn more from him than I could ever teach you," he told us.

I no longer needed a computer to see that at bat in Atlanta on April 8, 1974, where he hit his 715th home run in front of 54,000 people, breaking Babe Ruth's record. It happened in the fourth inning with two outs and a man on first base. I would never fast-forward, though; somehow, that seemed like cheating. Dad always said that it was a whole game, a whole season, and ultimately an entire career that led up to an unforgettable moment. That there was no way you could cut corners and get there and that Hank Aaron's story exemplified this fact perfectly. So I felt that I absolutely needed to watch the whole game, see the way he played Al Downing (career ERA 3.22, 1639 SOs, 123–107 W–L), the veteran pitcher, and take notes on Aaron's patience, which was something I always needed to work on. I was never more my father's daughter than when my nose was an inch away from the screen as Hank Aaron stepped into the box.

But there were also other videos of Aaron a click away from the prescribed clip. In the sidebar of related videos, I found film from the early sixties with Aaron discussing removal of segregation signs and policies at the Milwaukee Braves' spring training facility in Bradenton, Florida. My favorite video (after the record-breaking game) was Hank explaining the hate letters he received from people around the country who didn't want him to break the record, just because he was black. Jason found this clip morbid; I could tell by the way his nose wrinkled up every time he heard the word "nigger."

"Dear Nigger Henry," Hank Aaron read to the camera, enunciating each word. "It has come to our attention that you are going to break Babe Ruth's record. I don't think that you are going to break this record established by the great Babe Ruth if I can help it. Getting back to your blackness, I don't think any coon should ever play baseball. Whites are far more superior than jungle bunnies. I will be going to the rest of your games and if you hit more than one home run it will be your last. My gun is watching your every black move. This is no joke."

Jason would slowly back out of the room whenever I played this one. If Dad was in the room, he'd focus on whatever magazine or scouting report was closest. I could sense their discomfort, but it didn't bother me. Sometimes when I watched that clip, I actually laughed, because Hank Aaron had done it anyway; people were threatening to kill him every time he went up to bat just because he was so good that he was going to break a record that a white man had happened to set. I was sure I could see it each time he stepped up to the plate; the laughter, which could also be my laughter, settling into the contours of his face. Though I had never faced what he had, I felt like I knew something about how he felt up there, how he just had to play, even though he himself might never know why.

I'm not stupid. I was just a little blind.

CHAPTER
NINE

The tub felt solid against my ass as I perched on its edge a week after Kit's odd dinnertime outburst. Warm water surrounded my calloused and tired feet. My wet hair sprayed out like a wild mane down my neck and onto my back. I had already used up a third of the new conditioner Mom had bought for me and Kit, lathering it everywhere. Soon I would have to pick my hair out—my least favorite part of bathing because it could take almost an hour. I might as well soak my feet at the same time. This was why I had placed a copy of *Americanah* on the floor beside me—a reading break from the frustration of my hair every twenty minutes or so. I had just read a passage that was now jammed in my brain, mostly because I felt like I was hovering on the edge of really grasping it:

> *The only reason you say that race was not an issue is because you wish it was not. We all wish it was not. But it's a lie. I came from a country where race was not an issue; I did not think of myself as black and I only became black when I came to America.*

I arched my back and stared up at the skylight. It was early evening, just before dusk, and the March sky was a cloudless blue, darkening slowly. I closed my eyes and let all the scenes from that day's game play across my eyelids: the shot out to center that should have been a home run but wasn't because I tracked it perfectly, jumped, and caught it; the line drive past second that I should have picked up fast; Jason's dismal at bats.

"Alex!"

I opened my eyes. The night was only a window above me; perhaps it didn't even exist on the other side.

"Alex!"

It sounded like Kit, but the water was so loud I couldn't tell for sure. I reached over and turned off the faucet. "I'm in here," I said, which was our family's code for *Get lost!*

"Shh!" hissed the voice on the other side.

I rolled my eyes. "You're going to have to wait," I said. "I can read to you later, but I just started soaking my—"

The door opened abruptly, and my wild-eyed sister appeared before me. She shut the door carefully behind her and stood there, clutching something in her right hand.

"What the hell?" I said, before I could help myself. I was sure I had locked the door. "Go bother Mom or something." I tightened the suddenly too-small towel across my chest.

"Shh!" she said again.

I groaned, rubbing my forehead. "I'm just trying to soak my goddamn feet, and I want you *out*. *Now*." I tried to make my voice as threatening as possible, but Kit just stepped closer.

"Here," she said, thrusting a worn envelope toward me.

I peered at the gray paper incredulously. "What is that?"

She stared at me but did not move. "It's yours."

I took in her faded overalls, her partially undone braids that almost hung to her shoulders. Who was this girl? Was she even still a girl, or had she grown up when I wasn't looking? I studied the envelope. It was addressed to me, but I didn't recognize the handwriting. There was no return address. I turned it over in my hands carefully, trying to weigh its import by its feel, its scent. It smelled old; that much was for sure.

"Where did you get this?" I asked her. She was my sister, but I didn't know what that meant anymore.

She pursed her lips and then crossed her arms on her chest. "It belongs to you, not to them," she said. "They want you—well, both of us, really—to not know ourselves so that we'll think that we're them. But we're not them. We're *us*."

I was getting more and more confused by the minute. "Look," I said slowly. "I'm not sure what you're trying to do, but—" The envelope slipped out of my damp fingers.

"He's your father," she blurted. *What if Alex's birth parents can teach her about black people, so maybe she wouldn't feel so . . .*

I felt my breath catch in the pit of my stomach. In the warm, salty water, my toes wiggled. I looked above me, and the night seemed to expand into emptiness everywhere. I turned toward Kit. "What?" I could barely get the word out.

She pursed her lips again. "Read it. He sent it five years ago. When you were eleven. My age."

I moved my legs out of the tub, onto the cold tile floor. I reached down and picked up the small, thin document again. This time, it felt delicate and tenuous between my fingers.

Kit opened the door and had almost slipped out again before I asked her where she had found it. "You know where," she said quietly. And I saw the den, the books piled to the ceiling, the files and files neatly stacked in cabinets. The bathroom door closed. Kit was gone. And I was surprised to find that I wasn't even angry at her.

My feet, though, were still throbbing and blistered. Dead skin was coming off the side of my left foot from calluses. I shivered and tightened the towel around me. I turned the envelope over in my hands.

I knew this much already: I had been adopted from the state home when I was five months old. I weighed 15 pounds and was 26 inches long. Ninety-eighth percentile. When my mother first held me, she said that I squirmed out of her arms, uncomfortable with the proximity, the heat of touch.

There was an uneven tear at the top of the envelope, ripped diagonally downward. The envelope had been opened, and the letter it contained, folded into eight perfect squares, slid out easily. I unfolded the paper slowly, and when I began to read it, the wind was almost knocked out of me.

Dear Alexandra,

(Alexandra. They had given me the name because they said that it meant "Defender of man," and also, "One who comes to save the warriors." He and Mom would laugh, and say that even then, as a baby, they knew I would be fierce.)

I don't know if you got the other letters I sent, so I'm just gonna keep on writing.

I'm not good at writing letters, I'm actually not any good at writing, but I want to write to you. I know it's not allowed, there are rules and everything, and that there are good reasons for the rules, but there are some things I just need to say.

I would like to meet you someday. I am your father. There was a lot of things that could have been better between your mother and I. I would have liked the chance to know you.

I seen the newspapers about your adopted father and your family. You all can really play baseball, I hear! I think that is wonderful. That is how I found you. You weren't too hard to find actually, it was almost like you were waiting for me to find you. It is a small world.

Did you know I don't even live too far away? Just in Detroit. Just a seven hour drive.

You and your parents don't need to worry about me showing up at your house one day, though—I would never do that. I just want to talk to you, even just once. But if I have to wait until you're grown, I can do that, too. It's just that I have already waited a lot of years.

Please write if you have the chance.

Love, your father,

Keith

I opened my mouth to say something, but no sound came out. *He sent it five years ago.*

"I would like to meet you someday."

"I just want to talk to you, even just once."

"There was a lot of things that could have been better between your mother and I."

I read the letter at least five more times in the antiseptic silence of the bathroom, while the bathtub faucet dripped behind me.

I had always known everything I needed to know about myself. Baseball player. Center fielder. .311/.403/.561. Honor Roll. 3.97. But now what had seemed like me felt insubstantial compared to what slid out of that envelope. To have the story, whatever story it was, whatever pieces were left out, to have all that laid out in front of me like this in imperfect, awkward cursive, and then to call it my father's story—what was I supposed to do with that? Reading it was like reading the newspaper or reading a novel; it almost had nothing to do with me at all. Almost.

I stood up suddenly and whipped the door open.

"Kit!" I screamed. I was aware that my voice sounded frantic in my ears, but when I didn't get any response, I screamed again. But there was no answer, none at all. The house was dead.

Mom was still at work at the Cultural Center, and Dad was driving Jason to a study session with some friends. *Yes, this is your family. This is where you live. You have a right to storm around this house in a towel, your hair becoming more of a disaster by the second.* I strode out into the hallway, walked to her room, and knocked on the door, which she always kept locked. But she was nowhere. Apparently, she had left immediately after her task had been completed.

It doesn't matter. I knew where she had found it, even if I didn't know how she had gotten a hold of it before me, or why. And I also knew there were other letters. I threw on my robe and ran to the den.

Glossy, grinning photographs of us kids watched me as I sped downstairs. I winced and stepped into the freezing cold, air-conditioned room filled with books on the history of baseball, books by baseball greats, books on various aspects of technique, and then the shelves and shelves of DVDs of Dad's games when he was at Clemson, in the minors, and finally with the Brewers. And there were hard drives with my games, Jason's games, West High's games. The bookshelves were actually built into the walls and stretched almost to the ceiling. When we bought the house, Dad had made remodeling the basement into his "den" his first priority, particularly building the shelves. He liked to be surrounded by the game and his own history with it.

What I was looking for would not be on those shelves. Instead, I found the dull gray file cabinet. An afterthought Dad had picked up when he realized there were things that couldn't go on display.

I shivered, holding my elbows in my hands. I knew what I was doing. I strode over to the file cabinet and began rifling through the hundreds of files inside it, with titles like "Mortgage papers 1999," "Health files—KIT," "Health files—JASON," "Car title," "Insurance policies," and "Taxes." My fingers couldn't move fast enough, touching each file's label for a second, then flying on, trying to find the one that had to be there, the one I had been avoiding all my life without even knowing it. "Alex—ADOPTION." My fingers stopped finally, pulling out the thick yellowing folder and studying it carefully once it was in my hands.

It was frayed at the edges, like someone had accidentally spilled some water on it and the years had done the rest. Its title was scrawled in light pink marker, the letters elegantly separated in my mother's tall, distinctive print. I sat down, or fell down on the floor, the tiles biting into my tailbone. I sighed; the folder had been here all along. I took a deep breath and opened it. A faded letter lay on top.

Family and Child Services
Suite 326, 500 Main St.
Milwaukee, WI 53201

Mr. and Mrs. Terrence Kirtridge
15 Glendale
Milwaukee, WI 53204

February 17, 1999

Dear Mr. and Mrs. Kirtridge:
We are happy to inform you that your application to adopt a child with "special needs" through our agency has been formally accepted. We will do our utmost to place a child in your home as soon as possible.
In the meantime, if you have questions or concerns, please feel free to contact our office.
Sincerely,
Francis Hayes, ACSW
Director

ADOPTION FEES
Adoption fees will be based on our actual cost for providing the service as explained in the group meeting you attended. Actual cost of service per placement in 1997 was $3,000.00.
Fees will normally be paid within the calendar year that the child is placed.

The paper shook in my right hand, and I gripped my wrist with my left hand to steady it. I was a child with "special needs"? What the hell did that mean? Had I been walking around for all these years with some hidden malady that my parents hadn't bothered to tell me about? And then there was the fact that I cost three thousand dollars. It was not a small amount of money back then, but it was also not a particularly large one, if what you got for it was a child. Of course, I knew, way back in my brain, that some kind of transaction had resulted in me becoming part of my family, but to have it laid out so bluntly in front of me made my stomach turn. At the end of the day, I was something that could be bought and sold, like soap in the supermarket. Like a baseball player on a rookie deal. I was a child, but I was also a product.

There were at least twenty envelopes stacked behind the paper. I picked up the first one, which read "Ms. Alexandra Kirtridge" across the front and had a post date of August 10, 2010. The handwriting matched that on the letter that Kit had given me. The letter slid out as easily as the first one had, its words as labored and sincere. He had sent me letters for three years; one every other month. They were all in the folder. Each one said that he thought about me every day and that he hoped I was doing well. He had started writing when I was eleven and had finally given up, it appeared, when I was fourteen. Either he guessed that my parents were hiding the letters from me, or he figured I wasn't interested in meeting him.

Dear Alexandra,

Did you get my other letter? How are you?

Dear Alexandra,

How has fall been treating you? The leaves are just starting to turn here. It is beautiful.

Dear Alexandra,

This will be my last letter to you in awhile. I think I sent enough. Hopefully some day, when you're ready, we can see each other. I am thinking of you and wishing your family the best.

Love,

Keith

A hot tear from my eye blurred the carefully written cursive in the letter, and I threw the last letter to the floor. I pulled my knees to my chest and began rocking back and forth. My chest felt like it was full of fluid. Mucus gathered in my mouth and mingled with tears saturating my lips and I debated whether or not to spit all of it out onto the elegantly tiled floor. Instead I swallowed and then felt a wave of nausea wash over me. At 3:15 every afternoon, it was either me or Dad who walked out of our brightly lit foyer, onto the stone walkway lined by sunflowers and tulips that Mom diligently tended, and down to the white metal mailbox to get the mail. If I got it, I would sift through it—carefully if I was just relaxing in the house, hurriedly if I had other things to do—my attention singularly focused on anything baseball-related. It was true that I didn't always inspect every piece meticulously. But how could I have missed twenty letters from my birth father, even over a period of years?

Mom and Dad must have felt like I couldn't handle that kind of information when I was so young. That must have been their reasoning for not showing me the letters. *That's nobody's business but ours.* I pulled my legs tighter to my chest so that I could barely feel their circulation. My throat tightened further. *But they still should have told me. How could they have kept it from me?*

I turned away from the filing cabinet and saw myself. The one break in the built-in bookshelves was for a floor-to-ceiling mirror. After a film session, Dad didn't want us to have to go far to start applying corrections to our mechanics, so I'd spent hours in front of that mirror with a bat in my hand. I was a slightly open-stance hitter with fast hands and a swing that took a long, smooth cut through the zone. Maybe I wasn't powerful, but I would make good contact. The mirror had shown me that thousands of times. Now, I saw a scared girl who may have been faking it on the field and in front of the plate the whole time. A girl who only got the long, hard hits, who caught all those rogue fly balls because she listened to her father, who was now a confirmed liar. And the worst part about this girl was that she was only realizing this now. Paddington's thick, hot tongue licked my face clean. I hadn't even heard him come into the room. He wagged his tail.

"Hi," I said, and he wagged his tail more.

I scratched behind his ears, and he sat down lazily, eager to accommodate me. "Good boy," I said, and then I pushed myself up, back onto my haunches. I gathered the letters together and stacked them up neatly in the folder, the way I had found them. If secrets were what this family kept, then I could keep my own. I stood up and dusted myself off. The folder should go back in the drab gray filing cabinet; no one except Kit needed to know I had seen it.

I spotted the family photo hanging on the downstairs wall and stood on tiptoe in order to inspect it. Jason was smiling brightly in the photo but a little too carefully, the checkered sweater vest Mom had picked out for him sagging over his trim adolescent torso. I stood beside him, a little bit behind him actually, my wild hair pulled back into a somewhat tame bun, a dowdy violet dress hiding most of me. I looked into my eyes, and they were carefree, without any hint that something was amiss. I was surprised to notice that I envied that girl, even though I didn't want to be her now. To her right stood Kit, quietly clasping her hands, her mouth in a tight thin line, her eyes looking into the camera questioningly. Mom and Dad perched behind the three of us, Mom's torso turned a bit to the right, and Dad's facing the camera straight-on. Mom looked as happy as she always did, her right hand placed on Kit's shoulder, probably at rest after stroking and fixing Kit's long blonde hair. She could never do the same with my curls, which had a mind of their own, so by this time she hardly ever touched them anymore. Dad's arms stretched wide around us all, and his face was just *satisfied*. That was the word that came to mind, and as it entered my consciousness and attached itself to Dad, so did a fierce anger that made me want to break the picture entirely. Instead I dug around in one of Dad's desk drawers and found a Sharpie. I approached the photo gingerly this time, uncapping the marker and trying to imagine what my birth father might look like. When the marker touched the surface of the glass, I felt free for just a moment, drawing a figure slightly taller than Dad, standing right behind him. A shadow. I could see him, just barely, with curly hair, a mustache, and high, defined cheekbones. I stood back and stared for a moment. I could still wipe it away, but after a minute, I decided to leave the shadow there, for everyone to find it, and for no one, as well.

CHAPTER
TEN

Mom has her, deep in the belly. Tables and chairs and ends of things come at Mom. She is too round. Her whole body pink when she gets up or down. Always saying, *Terry, can you bring me an old washcloth? Terry, can you make me a thick vanilla shake with melon and cantaloupe?* Dad running in the house, up the stairs, in the kitchen, to the store. I like to go with him to get things for my little baby sister who is coming.

Alex, I have to get something for Mom, he says, bending so that he is small like me. *I don't have time to play with you right now.* I want to play Tonka trucks. Either that or Big Wheels.

I pull on the ends of his moustache until he takes my hands. This is a game we play. *But I can help,* I say. *I can wet the washcloths; I can carry the melon.*

Jason begins to cry because Dad won't play. He's acting like such a baby.

Terry, I'm so hot . . . she says from the couch. She is wearing a wavy white dress, the sound of the same words every day at the same time. She does not change, except for getting bigger and louder. Even with my sister in her, she is empty, and we can't make her full.

Dad looks at her and then at Jason and me, sweating. Since our family is being made, we are starting to grow into people, and Dad is always tired. But also smiling. He presses my hands harder and whispers in my ear. *Little Kirtridge*, he says, *I almost forgot that I do need your help at the supermarket. I need you to pick out the roundest, sweetest cantaloupe for your mother.*

I clap my hands together and jump up. Dad stands up, looking for his wallet so we can go. His arm muscles are strong and bursting from his T-shirt. Baseball has made him this way. When he reads to me, I touch his arms. His muscles are the hills and valleys of his body.

Jason can help, too, I say, turning to him and grabbing his cheeks. Then I kiss Jason, wet and hard on the lips, and say, *I love you*. Jason starts to smile and Dad says, *Well, all right then*. Jason would be so sad without me.

When we are in the car, on our way to Kroger's, I whisper to Jason, *You love me best of all. Best of anyone. I'm your sister.*

He is four and loves his own jokes. *I'm your sister*, he says, hitting his chest.

I laugh. *No, no*. Me, I say, pointing to my chest. *Sister.*

Dad looks back at us, from the front seat. *But you'll be getting another sister soon*, he says. *In two months.*

Jason and I stare at each other. I grab his fingers and he screams. Dad frowns. *Jason!*

I let go of his fingers, and Jason closes his mouth and smiles.

What's her name, Dad? I ask.

Your mother and I are still deciding between Danielle and Katherine. What do you guys think?

I want to think hard, so I put my head in my hands like Dad when there is a big thought in it. *Katherine*, I say. *Katherine is better.*

Our car comes into the parking lot. *You think so?*

I nod. *Yes,* I say. *If I have a sister, she should be called Katherine.*
Dad laughs, a laugh I do not like. *Why do you say that?*

I lean to him. *Dad. Will Katherine be coming from the same place I came from?*

I hold the story in my mind, the one that Mom tells me sometimes before bed, the one that Dad tells me more. A woman is going to have a baby, but she is poor and she is sad and she has no money to take care of the baby. She doesn't know how she will feed it, buy it clothes, take it to the doctor. The father is also poor and does not know how to take care of the baby. He and the woman don't love each other, so they can't get married, which the baby will need to be taken care of properly. So, the woman decides to find a home for the baby where the parents can take good care of it, where they will love it as much as she and the father do. The baby is born in the hospital, and after it is born, the woman gives it to the couple. This is what happened to you. It makes you special because it means that we really wanted you, that we picked you out ourselves because you were so special.

More special than Jason? No, not more special than Jason. Equally special. *How can we be equally special if he just came out of you and you picked me out?* He didn't just come out of us, we made him out of love. We made him together. *But you didn't make me together.* No, your birth mother and father made you together. *But they didn't make me out of love. They made me out of something else.* They did make you out of love. But sometimes love doesn't last. *Why did you pick me then?* I told you. Because you're special.

Will we get to pick Katherine out? I can see the babies in tiny cribs beside each other. There would be ones with curly brown hair like mine and tiny big toes. We can pick one with holes in her cheeks when she smiles.

Dad frowns. *Alex, you know your mother's pregnant. You know where your sister's coming from.* We are stopped in the car now. In a minute, we will walk into Kroger's.

She is not empty, I see now; there is something inside her.

Katherine will be pushing out soon enough. Like Jason, she will not be picked out.

I unbuckle Jason's seatbelt. *Katherine will be born from Mom*, I say slowly.

Jason gets down from his car seat. Dad comes over to help us. *You know, I never said that her name was Katherine, Alex. I said that we're thinking about Katherine or Danielle.*

I step away from him, cross my arms. *You'll choose Katherine*, I say. *That's her name.*

Dad was about to take my hand, but I'll never forget the way he stopped after I said that, the strange gaze he gave me. I like to think that he began to realize that I could create her just as much as he and Mom could, that I was already a part of who she was even before she was born. I would find a way to choose her, one way or another.

I got away from him and put my arm through Jason's. We were halfway to the front of the store before he caught us.

...

They put Jason's old baby crib near me, and Dad pushes my bed in the corner. They pile my toys on one side of the room.

She'll be very delicate, Mom tells me at bedtime. *You'll have to be very careful with her.*

Careful is ugly to me. Why can't she stay in Jason's room? I ask. *That's the baby room. This is the big kid room.*

Mom's face is beside me, laughing. *Jason's just a year younger than you; he doesn't have the baby room.* Her soft, shiny hair tickles my chin. I want to touch it. It is clean and slippery in my hands until she takes it away. *I'm sorry, that hurts, honey.* She sighs. Will it be like taking a pin to a big balloon when she goes to the hospital? Will she just pop like that? Everyone says that Katherine is inside her, but how? No person, even so small, could fit there. If it *is* true, Mom will shove her out, or she will shove herself out of Mom. Like a war, where each good guy wants to get away from the other. *It'll be fine*, she says. *You know, I always wanted a sister to play with when I was a girl.*

I stick my fingers under my butt. I have to stop them from pulling on her hair again. *Well, why didn't you, then?*

She razzes my head. *Because I didn't have one, silly. You know it's just me and Uncle Eddie.*

I feel stupid. I look away from her, outside into the dark.

She'll look up to you, your sister. She'll need you and you'll need her. Plus, you'll be able to tell her things that you could never tell Jason. She looks at me, almost sad. *That's what's so great about having a sister.*

Is she really talking to me? Would she even notice that I was gone if I floated away and left only my head peeking out from the covers? No. She would never know the difference.

...

But when my sister arrives, nothing is the same. The house turns green with flowers and potted plants, then red with candies, then pink with visitors. I like it in Jason's room, playing Lincoln Logs and reading him stories. The baby is tiny and soft and hardly ever makes a sound. Everyone who comes says she is the sweetest baby they have ever known. When Grandma Jordan meets the baby, she asks me if I don't feel like the luckiest girl in the world. She hands me a soft caramel and I nod.

But on the inside, really I hate the baby. Late at night, when everyone sleeps, I jump out of bed and watch her chest move up and down, her eyelids swish-swash back and forth. Her toes twitch as she sleeps, and her hands grab at nothing. I lean down to her, so my face is almost touching hers, and I breathe on her. I blow back air I save in my lungs for her, air which is *bad*. Then I pinch her little ears and pull the thin, white hairs around her head. Sometimes, she wakes up screaming, and Mom rushes in, asking, *What's wrong? What happened? Is she hungry?* I throw my pillow over my head and pretend that I heard none of it, that sharing a room with my sister is the worst thing that has ever happened and will ever happen to me. *I don't know what is wrong with her,* I tell Mom.

It makes no difference, of course. She stays.

Then one night, I am asleep and I see rows and rows of baby cribs in the hospital. I am walking there, in my sister's baby clothes, and I am thinking I am going to pick one out; I am going to pick out a baby for myself. I tell them that I just want to pick one of them to take home, but they say no, that I already have a sister. I open my eyes. My hands are pee pee wet. The ceiling above me white, the fan still making circles in the corner. Tomorrow I will go to kindergarten and draw and play with the other kids, even though this is exactly what I did the day before. No day will be different from another, except for the fact that I *feel* different. Right at that moment, I know I am another person than I was even a moment before; I also know that no one will be able to understand this if I told them. *I am different.* I flex my hand. *The white fear. It's coming for me.* That is what I name it. The ceiling above me white, the fan still making circles in the corner. Tomorrow I will go to kindergarten and draw and laugh with the other kids, even though this is exactly what I did the day before. *This is all there is,* says my mind, or some-one in it. And the thought is an echo, repeating into nothingness. *This is all there is.* I touch a hand to my leg, and I know that it isn't real, that I am not real. *This is all there is. This can't be.* The walls and the ceiling make a storm around my head, and yet, they keep me here. Someone opens my mouth. I hear a short shout. From who? For what? Another cry is coming, but I know I cannot let this one come out. Mom or Dad might hear, and then what? They will come and ask what's wrong, and there will be nothing to say. I pull off the sheets and run to my sister's crib. She is lying there with no sounds, but her eyes are open. She has heard me.

Her big gray eyes, small storms themselves, holding me. What is in *her* mind? Am I *her* sister? The swirling pulls back, the echo moves on.

Did you hear it, too? I ask her.

But she doesn't answer. She keeps looking at me. What does she see?

I reach in and touch beside her eyes with my finger. She grabs onto it, so hard that I am scared.

God, I whisper. *You're strong.* I find the footstool in the corner, move it beside the crib, step up, and climb in. Then I put my hand on her back and another at her neck. They told me many times to never pick her up. *One, two, three*, I say, and lift her slowly. My eyes never leave hers. She fits into my arm, and I begin to rock her. She makes a *ca-ca-goo* sound and moves her feet.

You're Katherine, I whisper in her ear. *You're Kit.*

CHAPTER
ELEVEN

She was hunched over a book on Frida Kahlo the next morning, knees folded into her chest on our front steps. It was a thick, hardcover book that Grandma Kirtridge had given her for Christmas, and it looked like her tiny, delicate hands could barely hold it up.

"Good morning," I said, as I sat down next to her.

Kit peered at me sideways, her eyes slowly coming into focus. "Oh! Good morning!" she said, a little too brightly. It was almost like she had forgotten that I lived there, too, and that she would therefore probably run into me sooner rather than later.

Mrs. Olson waved as she passed us, and we waved back, absently.

"How's Frida?" I asked Kit, squinting into the sunlight.

"Who?" She closed the book, looking confused.

"You know, Frida," I said, pointing to the self-portrait of a young, all-too-prescient woman on the cover.

"Oh!" Kit laughed. "She's . . . not well, I believe. Streetcar crash rammed a steel rod and all her insides together, and she's never been the same since."

I nodded, remembering the story from when I had read it years ago, in some book I checked out from the library. It was a terrible accident that required her to wear a full body cast and endure multiple operations that were never really successful. She was in pain for the rest of her life. "Poor Frida," I said.

"Yeah," said Kit. She put the book down beside her. "But she learned something from the pain, I think."

"And what was that?"

Her eyes met mine, and I could see that she was tentative, scared. "She learned that she could live with it . . . if she could find a way to express it."

I grimaced. "Sounds pretty morbid."

Kit fiddled with her fingers. "You know she was mixed too, right? White and Mexican and Indian."

I scowled. "I don't even know what that means, anyway. Mixed." I sighed. "As far as I can tell, it means closer to white for Mom and Dad, and the lightest shade of black for everyone else."

Kit tried again. "All I'm trying to say is that all those letters, all that information—it's your story to have and do with what you wish." She scowled. "I just hated the way Mom and Dad were keeping it from you."

"What if they were trying to just keep me safe? Did you ever think of that?"

She glared at me. "Come on, Alex."

I looked down at my hands until I was ready to meet her eyes again. "I just don't understand why you felt the need to get involved in something that doesn't concern you."

She looked me up and down slowly, assessing me and my level of anger, perhaps. "If you're trying to tell me that I shouldn't have done it, that you're mad, I understand." She peered down the street, like she was trying to see something. "I'm just . . . worried about you."

I tried to laugh. "Well, you shouldn't be. I'm fine. Better than fine, actually. I'm one of the top high school center fielders in the country, probably about to win a state championship. And I've got a shot at valedictorian. Doesn't exactly sound like someone you should worry about, does it?"

Kit scowled. "That's Dad talking."

"Kit," I said wearily, standing up to go. "What do you want from me?"

She grabbed my hand. "I want you to talk to me." She looked at me, almost in desperation. "I need you to talk to me."

I sighed. "We talk all the time."

She squeezed my hand and looked me in the eyes, meaningfully.

I pulled my hand away. "I can't . . . talk about that yet."

She stood up and nodded like she understood, but I could tell the conversation wasn't over.

CHAPTER TWELVE

I think that Dad sensed that something was off, that Kit was getting to me, so he took me to Elle's, our favorite bagel shop, for lunch that weekend. They had lox and herring to die for. Dad's side of the family was originally from Brooklyn (though he'd grown up on Long Island), so he could never eat just any old bagel. Elle's was really the only bagel place Dad would venture to in Madison. Trips there were usually reserved for our annual father-daughter birthday lunch. It felt strange to be there on just a normal Saturday afternoon.

"So, so good," Dad said, wiping his mouth with a napkin. He had just bitten into a toasted garlic-onion bagel with cream cheese and lox. "It's been too long."

I forced a smile.

He could see that something was wrong. "Aren't you going to eat?" He pointed at my bagel plate of the day, which I hadn't touched.

I shrugged. "I'm not really hungry." I sat back in my chair and folded my arms across my chest. We had sat at this very same table, near the back by the south window, the same day every year since I could remember. Everything was always the same. Except for today.

Dad frowned. "That doesn't sound like you."

I stifled a grin. He often said that I could eat my weight, which was almost not an exaggeration. People always found my appetite confusing, since up to now I had always been excessively skinny.

"Alex," he said, after taking a deep breath. "I know you must have felt . . . awkward . . . at dinner the other night."

I couldn't look him in the eyes, so I looked out the window instead at all the people crossing the street to the farmer's market. *You are a liar. A liar.*

"I mean, I felt awkward, and I wasn't even in your shoes."

Good thing you know that your shoes are different from mine. I just kept staring out the window like there was something incredible out there that I couldn't afford to miss.

"You know, I just wish there were things I knew how to talk about with you," he said, warily.

That got my attention, and I looked him straight in the eyes. He was sad and the lines in his face seemed deeper somehow.

"Your mother and I . . . We have always just wanted to give you things. I mean, give you everything, really. Color never mattered to us, what anyone else thought never mattered to us." He sighed. "All we wanted was the best for you kids."

Did he know? I probed his eyes and decided that he didn't—at least consciously.

He rubbed his forehead. "I can't apologize for your sister—"

"There's nothing to apologize for," I said, surprising myself. The sharp edge in my voice made both us of flinch.

"Well, I wouldn't put it that way . . ."

"I would." I picked up my cinnamon apple bagel and took a huge bite out of it. Maybe that would stop me from talking.

Dad sighed. "Look, Alex."

I chewed on my bagel noisily and pretended that my eyes were closed. I could almost see the black of my eyelids everywhere.

"The way that conversation about your . . . *identity* . . . came about was all wrong. Anyone could see that. But at the same time . . ." He paused and appeared to be thinking for a minute. "I think that Kit had a good point about what an awkward position you're in sometimes, in terms of the assumptions people make about you. I had never really thought about that before."

I forced myself to swallow. The breath in my windpipe was getting tighter, and I sensed that hiccups were well on their way.

Dad leaned forward, his brow furrowed, and took my small hand in his large one, as he'd done so many times before when we were having difficult conversations about my game, school, friends, or even family. His thumb rubbed my knuckles, which was usually a calming and reassuring gesture. "I just want you to know that your mother and I, we will always see you as just you, as Alex. There's nothing black—or particularly . . . racial—about you to us because you're our little girl and always will be."

Something about the way he said "black" made me cringe a little. Like it was the worst thing a person could be. I remembered his tone when he used the word "mixed" to describe me, however, and in contrast, it was almost prideful. Dad gave me a hesitant, crooked smile, which let me know that he was taking a risk, and saying things he hadn't intended to say to me, in an effort to make me okay again. And I should have appreciated this, even after what they had kept from me. Instead, I hiccupped and pushed my crossed ankles below the table together tighter and tighter.

"I know, Dad." As I said this, it was like there was another person saying it, standing outside my body—a robot almost, who knew exactly what to say, how, and when to say it, in order to affect the desired results.

Dad squeezed my hand, which was my signal that things were better now.

I feigned a smile, but my grip on his hand felt loose and undecided—like it could fall off at any minute and it wouldn't have mattered.

CHAPTER THIRTEEN

I threw myself into my school-work, which wasn't hard since the sophomore year honors track wasn't exactly easy and there were a lot of projects toward the end of the year. I was also dragging Jason to the batting cage whenever I had the chance. Neither of us wanted to bring up Kit, so it was pretty easy to just talk about other things.

But I couldn't quite forget. More than once, I caught a glimpse of the gray filing cabinet out of the corner of my eye when I passed by the den, and my pulse would quicken. I'd feel the coarseness of the papers between my fingers, and I'd see the messy handwriting of the man who said he was my father. I couldn't help worrying that someone would throw them out, and then they would be gone—all that was left of my connection to my father and the only part of my mother I would ever know. But then I would blink and turn back toward the kitchen. I would see the glasses and perhaps the orange juice carton held tight in Jason's grasp. He would be discussing his batting stance with Dad, and then they would both laugh suddenly, and then I would be right there, in that precise moment, thinking, *This is your father. This is your brother. Your family.* I would step forward, toward them, into the kitchen, and the letters would be gone again, and all of it would be enough. At least for a moment.

•••

"You see the way he hits the ball *hard* at every at bat," Dad told Jason and me as we watched a game between the Mariners and the Red Sox in mid-Apri. He was talking about David Ortiz.

"That's a sign of greatness. I used to hit like that," Dad said wistfully. "That's why his home runs are always long line drives to straightaway right rather than fly balls that arc." Then he flipped a popcorn kernel into his mouth.

Jason nodded, peering at the screen intently. "Reminds me of Willie Mays," he said.

Dad looked at him suddenly, eyebrows raised. "Damn right."

The two of them reached into the popcorn bowl at the same time and grabbed huge fistfuls. It had only been a month since Jason had revealed his misgivings about the game to me at the pizzeria, but it already seemed like a distant memory—something he had said to me in a dream rather than real life.

Dad moved on to the relative weakness of Boston's pitching and defense, and I relaxed into the easy pattern of their conversation. Soon, Dad would start in on Pedro Martinez, and Jason would know exactly how to steer Dad toward his one Pedro at bat story (past-his-prime Pedro with the Mets, but still). I had just taken a sip of my Powerade when Mom peeked around the corner. "I need to see you in the kitchen," she said. Her small blonde head was barely visible in my line of sight, but her demeanor caught my attention. Something was on her mind. I groaned. I was just getting into the game. "Go ahead," I replied, fixing my eyes back on Ortiz. "I can talk and watch at the same time."

"It's really important." I caught an edge of something—I didn't know what—in her voice.

Ortiz swung and the ball thumped into the catcher's mitt.

"Oh!" said Dad and Jason, slapping their knees.

I rose from the couch slowly, carefully negotiating the glasses we had placed on the table. "Ma, I was wa—" I said, as I walked into the kitchen. But when I saw her face, I shut up—it was red and puffy, streaked with tears.

"Alex," she said, in almost a whisper. "I found this."

She held up the folder. I watched a few of the letters spill out, onto the countertop. I had to hold myself back from snatching those precious documents into my hands. She was cooking something on the stove, soup it smelled like, and the only sound in the room was its bubbling.

"That's . . . that's a folder," I said, feeling my face color. She might as well have been holding a baggie of meth for all the tension that suddenly filled the room. I didn't know what to do—would it even work to say that I had never seen the folder before?

Mom's face crumbled, and she dropped the folder onto the floor. "I knew you'd been in it! Everything was out of order," she said. And I thought I had put everything back just the way it was. My mother always was an expert observer of detail, though. "I wanted to just burn them, but your father wouldn't let me . . ." her voice trailed off, and she sank to the floor.

I rushed toward Mom, wrapped my arms around her. I had never seen her like this. "Mom, I didn't . . ."

She cupped my face in her hands. "Don't lie to me, Alexandra. I know you've been reading those letters," she said. *Should have been more careful*, I thought. But the shame was all twisted with anger. Why did they make me think first of preserving their comfort? I tried not to, but I had to break her stare.

"Which ones did you read?" she asked.

I looked down. I wished I could just melt into the floor. I wanted to tell her it wasn't any of her business anyway, that those letters didn't belong to her. "I don't know. I just wanted to see . . ." The note of apology in my voice and the smell of burning soup turned my stomach.

"Look at me!" she said. "I *am* your mother, right?" Tears streamed down her cheeks and her gray eyes flashed. "We know what's best for you, your father and I."

I was suddenly aware of Dad and Jason in the doorway. "Rachel," Dad said. "What the hell . . ."

Mom dropped my face abruptly and pushed herself up off the floor to face him. "She found the letters, Terry," she said.

Dad looked from me to Mom, incredulously.

"Yeah, that's right," Mom said. She wiped her eyes with the back of her hand. "The letters you told me there was no way she would ever find till she was ready!" she screamed. Then she turned back to me. "Well, does she look ready?"

I scrambled to my feet as three sets of eyes assessed me.

Mom whipped around, back toward Dad and Jason. "She's sixteen years old, Terrence! She's just a baby!" She covered her eyes with her hands. "And if that man gets a hold of her and starts telling her things she's not prepared to process . . . I've always known there is that biological connection that could pull her . . ."

That man.

Mom sank to the floor again, collapsing in sobs. Dad was at her side in one leap and rocking her in his arms. In the doorway, Jason's face was white. I took a step back but landed right up against the wall. I looked around. *I need to get out of here.*

"Alex," Dad said. "Come." He was using the gentle tone he always used to calm Mom. I didn't want to come, but my legs somehow shuffled over to them.

Mom was still sobbing, although her small frame was no longer racked by them. *You made her like this.*

"We did it for your own good," said Dad, speaking over the mess of Mom's hair. "It's against the law, what he did, contacting you like that." His voice was laced with anger. "It could be really

63

damaging for someone as delicate as you to get information like that before you're ready."

Someone as delicate as you. I couldn't for the life of me understand who they were talking about. I was many things, but we all knew that delicate wasn't one of them. *They're playing this one a little too hard.* And yet, I knew they weren't playing at all.

Mom grabbed my hand. Her palm was cold and wet and small.

"There was a reason why they took you from him," Dad was saying. "I know this is hard for you to hear, Alex, but you need to, because if you don't, you could really find yourself in trouble later. This man could be unstable. He could . . . take advantage of you if you let him." He took my other hand, so that we were one, large, pulsating blob of flesh on the kitchen floor.

"We've talked about this . . . mostly in harmless terms, but we've still talked about . . . the reasons why people give their children, and in your case, their five-month-old baby, up for adoption. Who would do it, if they could avoid it?" Dad continued.

I nodded. There was always some part of me that wondered why my mother and father had given me up, but a bigger part of me didn't really want to know.

Dad sighed. "Your mother was right that we should have gotten rid of those letters a long time ago. I just kept them because I felt it was the right thing to do. Maybe when you were better prepared for what you might find . . . An adult, at least."

With this, Mom let out an absolute howl and squeezed my hand so hard I thought it would break off.

What could possibly be so bad about him?

"I'm not going to contact him, okay?" I hated the person saying those words. *I need to get out of here.* I let go of Mom's hand and stood up. "I know enough now." *I don't know anything.* I looked over at the tattered folder, and its contents, littered across the floor. "I know enough." *You could really find yourself in trouble later.*

Mom buried her face in Dad's shoulder, and he rubbed her back. "It's okay," he told her softly. "It's okay now."

It will never be okay.

I wanted her to burn the letters. I wanted to say that he meant nothing to me. How could I tell them that *they* were my parents— they had raised me, they had loved me all this time, that there was no one else in the world who had any right to me? But more than saying it, I wanted to feel it. And I didn't.

In the living room, the TV blared with the muffled cheers of fans. Someone must have hit a home run—there was no mistaking that particular sort of cheer. And just like that, the familiar day-dream fought its way to the surface: I would hit a home run some day in the majors, I would make sure of it. I still wanted to do all the things that Dad hadn't had the chance to do because his career got cut short and he had to focus the rest of his time and energy on Jason and me.

"Come on," Dad said, helping Mom up. He gestured to Jason, who looked like a statue in the doorway. Jason and I started walking toward the living room, Mom in tow. "Go get your sister," said Dad. "We're having family time at the game. We got three more innings to watch."

CHAPTER FOURTEEN

Hot Milwaukee summer and the cool of popsicles at the price of perpetually sticky fingers and carpet. "Everything is sticky!" Mom says, throwing up her hands.

Interleague game with the Twins. Dad's September call up and strong spring were turning heads. He'd been starting at first base and was batting second.

Jason and I are sitting too close to the huge new TV Dad bought with his first "Major League money, Rachel! We're going to make it." But Jason and I are more interested in the popsicles because Major League money hasn't replaced the minor league air conditioner that Mom is trying to get to blow something other than hot air.

Then the familiar crack, the one Jason and I already know like we know our names.

The camera pans to Dad, holding his glove open, anticipating the throw. The pitcher whips the ball toward him, but he's off balance from the sliding catch. Dad sees this, adjusts his position in a split second, and stretches down the first-base line, hoping to still bag the catch. Mike Perry is one hop from the base, running like a freight train, and determined to get on.

And then it happens. In some ways, it's still happening.

. . .

I know now that Dad's agent had made the most of his client's strong September the year before, turning it into a 1.5 million dollar one-year deal. And I also understand now that the Brewers saw a feel-good story in Terry Kirtridge—the thirty-one-year-old dad who'd never given up on his dream, not even after playing nearly a decade in the minors.

But I didn't understand any of that when I was sitting too close to our new TV that day. I just knew Dad was hurt. When Perry crashed into Dad and knocked his shoulder out of joint and the ball out of his glove, my stomach and my popsicle dropped. Dad hit the ground in high definition, and I screamed and dug my finger-nails into the flesh of my palms. Perry leaned over Dad and started talking to him. Dad didn't respond; he lay there, motionless. The Brewers' trainers ran out of the dugout and made their way toward first base.

The announcer said something about it being "a shame since the Brewers feel-good minor-league miracle was looking like he was headed for the DL." All the while Dad lay motionless on the ground. We watched in strained silence as the trainers leaned over Dad. Even without a close-up, you could see he was in agony. In the end, they had to take him away on a stretcher.

There's a clip of the whole thing up on YouTube that I still watch from time to time. You can see in the slow-mo that Perry was bound to run into Dad one way or another, that Dad had placed himself in a precarious position with his left shoulder blocking the base. I don't think that Perry would think twice about knocking him down if Dad was in his way. He was a professional ball player, after all—still is today. But even though Dad called, and still calls, Perry every swear word in the book, I never once believed that Perry would intentionally give him a chronic, career-ending injury. Who would want to go down on record as the man who busted Terry Kirtridge's shoulder so bad that he was never the same again? Who would want to go to bed knowing that you had effectively stopped someone's career at thirty-one?

• • •

Although he recovered enough to play the next season, Dad's performance was less than impressive in spring training. It was pretty clear that he wouldn't see the major league roster any time soon. He was thirty-two and had never done anything but play baseball.

In late September, he was offered a position of first-base coach for the Brewers AA team, in Huntsville, Alabama. He mulled over it for a week before he was asked to coach the top boys' middle and high school baseball teams in the state. The positions were at Cherokee Middle School and West High School.

"It's an opportunity," he said to Mom as he sat down at the kitchen table. "Look what I've done for our kids so far, just through coaching. I could do so much more with so many other kids."

Jason and I peered at each other from around the corner. It was the first time we had ever heard him talk about coaching anyone but us. And since he had not shown the least bit of interest in resuming our training since his injury, I felt a twinge of jealousy at the thought of him coaching others.

"I think you should take it, Terry," Mom said, shredding lettuce. "We could all use a change."

What she meant was that the teams were in Madison, so we'd have to move. We would have to sell the house, leave our friends, leave school, and everything in Milwaukee.

My stomach churned at the thought, for all the things I would push away and all the new things I would take in. I lay in bed every night those last few weeks with my palm pressed against the wall, trying to remember its coolness, imprint it in my memory. Because I knew that soon enough, my room and the wall would become only thoughts to me, images, as intangible as Dad's leaping catches on the field were to him now.

CHAPTER FIFTEEN

"Pickles," I said, handing Jason a regular-sized mason jar. Jason grabbed it and set it up on the shelf carefully.

"Sweet or garlic?" Jason asked.

I checked the label on the side of the jar where Mom's perfect handwriting identified the correct item. "Garlic," I said.

Canning was something my mother had grown up with, something she fell back on when she was stressed. When Mom and Dad's realtor found a house in Madison that had all the modern conveniences (and a yard big enough for a batting cage) but also the root cellar from the original farmhouse, Mom took it as a sign. The last of Dad's signing bonus more than covered the down payment.

For Jason and me, though, the cellar was a hated spring chore— taking inventory and organizing so Mom could begin to plan her purchases at Madison's overflowing farmer's markets.

Jason pushed a jar over to the left, raising a wave of dust from the rickety wood shelf.

I coughed. "Damn." I waved my hand.

"Sorry," he said.

"Doesn't anyone ever clean those?" I asked.

Jason snickered. "Yeah, and who's going to do it? You?" He reached over me and tried to grab another jar from the box.

"Hey," I said, pushing him aside. "I got it." The dust had settled now and I could breathe.

He stepped back. "Fine. Then let's hurry up and finish. I got things to do." A rectangular shadow played across his face, making him look angry.

I shivered and turned back to the box. It was half empty. Once this chore was done, I could go back to my reading, and he could go back to studying old DVDs of his at bats from last season when he was a .301/.366/.550 hitter. I leaned down and picked up the next jar. It was large and full of bright pink globs that were blinding even in the partial light.

"Ugh," said Jason, wrinkling his nose.

I turned it over in my palm. "It's beets," I said. "I guess they're pickled." I handed him the jar and he took it reluctantly.

"Won't catch me eating that anytime soon," he said, placing it on the left side of the shelf. "Those things look disgusting." He frowned and dusted off his hands.

I shrugged and picked up another jar of chili sauce. "Taste is different than look."

Even with his back to me, I could feel him glaring. He had been surly lately. I mostly tried to stay out of his way because I knew we were both edgier and edgier with each game West High won. At that precise moment, we were exactly four games away from being the top-rated team when we entered the state tournament. While Jason had just heard that he had made the cut for the elite club team where we would play through the summer and fall, I was still waiting to hear. So, I really didn't see what he had to be surly about at all. Everyone said that the elite club team was a direct pipeline to the best college ball, and if you had the gift

71

and grit, hopefully something even better, like the draft.

Jason took the chili sauce and shoved it to the right. The shelf sagged under the weight, but held. I grabbed a jar of green beans. There was nothing in the world as good as a freshly picked green bean, but if you couldn't get that, one from a jar that Mom had packed would do just fine. I closed my eyes for a second, remembering the sharp crunch of the bean skin in my mouth.

"You know, we're your real family," Jason said.

I turned the words over in my mind; I could not figure out what they meant. I turned to face him.

"Those other people gave you up years ago. Mom and Dad wanted you, and that's the end of it." He took the jar of green beans from me, but his eyes were hard and held my gaze. "At least, that's how I see it."

I hiccupped and desperately searched my mind for something to say and found nothing.

Jason turned toward me, so that I had to step back. "I don't know why you had to go and dig up those letters. You got Mom sad all the time, and Dad completely scattered." He placed the beans in the center of the shelves.

I broke away from his face, which was not the same face that had run cones and thrown long toss in practice with me for years, and looked down at my right hand. It was burnt deep brown by the May sun—my throwing hand. The part of me that knew how to think better than my brain most the time. The part of me that mattered most. That hand held no answer for this.

"I wish you had never found them," he said angrily.

"Why?" I said, finally finding my voice. "So you and Dad and Mom would feel better?"

Jason stepped back, and I felt like I could breathe again. "Alex, this isn't about anyone feeling better. It's about reality. I've never seen you as black and neither has Mom or Dad or Kit, okay?"

I had heard those same words come out of Mom and Dad's mouths so many times before, but hearing it from Jason for the first time made my knees shake. For some reason, a tidal wave was building in my stomach and crashing in my ears. It felt like my body was on the verge of exploding in on itself, of disappearing under the weight of all that people didn't think of me as. It was too much. I thrust my index finger in his face, and he looked scared of me, really scared, for the first time in years. It felt good to see him flinch. "You have no idea how I'm seen, got it?"

Before I was conscious of what I was doing, my throwing hand swung at him, making contact with his jaw. I yelped in pain as I heard my knuckles crack against bone. He recovered quickly, grabbed my wrists, and ran me back against the wall, pinning my arms against the brick wall. The wind knocked out of me, I felt my hand scrape against the sharp limestone. I tried to push back, managing to get my bleeding right arm away from the wall by a few inches, but it was useless—he really was stronger than me now. His arms strained against his T-shirt, and he was half-grinning as he began to twist my right arm. Yes, he was coming at me hard, and all I could manage at the moment was just to take it, to bite back the cry growing in my throat. *Come on. Come on!* my brain screamed, the same mantra I said when a ball was headed my way during a game and I needed that highest level of concentration. But there was no denying that I already *was* on that level, and all I could manage was to release the growling howl in the back of my throat, as a bolt of red energy ran up my arm. I didn't even recognize the sound as it came out of me.

Then it was like Jason woke up or something. His eyes opened wide, and he let go of me. I slid down the wall to the ground, still howling, but dully.

Even though my hand and arm throbbed, it felt good to lie on the dark, wet floor, to let the cool seep into my bones and calm them. I held onto my knees and tried to make myself as small as possible. Eventually, the pain dulled, and I found I could speak again. "I said I wouldn't touch those letters again," I said quietly.

Jason had moved to the other side of the room by that time and was sitting on the stone steps, holding his head in his hands. He lifted it up for a moment and squinted at me. "What?"

I sat up and touched my fist with my left hand. It was swollen and bleeding lightly, but it was nothing serious. "I don't want to know what my birth father wrote," I said. "Mom and Dad were right. I know I'm not ready." I pushed myself up from the floor a bit unsteadily. *I would like to meet you someday. I am your father.*

Jason came to my side and braced my side with his own weight. "I'm sorry. You know I didn't mean to do that."

I nodded. "I know." And I *did* know. I knew he was my brother, and I knew with a sudden stab of sadness that we would never be as close as we had been in the past. We headed toward the stairs, taking very slow, very tiny steps together.

"Don't tell Mom," we both said at the same time. Then we laughed, a strained sort of laughter. We took the first step carefully, negotiating both weight and space. I told him that I had it after that one and made it up the steps just fine on my own. When we got to the top, we both had our usual pleasant looks plastered across our faces. No one would be able to tell that nothing was the same.

CHAPTER
SIXTEEN

Since Jason and I never spoke of the incident in the cellar again, it was almost like it hadn't even happened. Almost, but definitely not exactly. My throwing arm and hand had completely healed two weeks later, the body forgetting almost as fast as the mind, moving on to new concerns. Which was how I could find myself completely engrossed at Foot Locker not long after that in search of new cleats. My screw-ins were almost completely worn down, and in the game that week I'd failed to track down a fly ball because I'd slipped on my first step.

Buying the shoes on my own was in itself a small act of defiance—a crack in the Kirtridge family monolith that only one of us could notice. First, Dad was an absolute Nike man (he'd been close to a small endorsement deal when the collision happened). Second, buying equipment without his oversight was just not done.

But I knew how to read shoe reviews as well as he did and Nike cleats had always been a little too wide for me anyway.

I turned over a pair of Mizuno 9-Spikes in my hands. I knew

now that Mizunos ran narrow and so I only needed to find a sales-person to see if they also came in my size and in red.

"Alex?" A voice said in back of me. In an instant, I recognized it. I felt my face color, and I whipped around. *Reggie.*

He was standing right there, a big grin on his face. His fore-head was broader than I remembered; his eyes kinder.

"Yeah, yes," I stammered. "Nice to see you again." *Girl, you can play some ball.* It was late May now, two months since that at bat. One month since we had battled, plate to mound, and I had won. And two months since he had caught me lying about my family.

"How you doing?" he said.

I must have looked completely bewildered because he went on. "It's Reggie," he said. "Reggie Carter."

I looked up at him sharply. "I know," I said. "I remember you. The killer fastball. Not something I could forget too easily."

He grinned and crossed his arms in front of him. His whole body lit up when he smiled—like he was a completely different person, almost. "Naw, I guess not," he said. Little crinkles formed around his eyes.

I tried to smile.

"No one forgets you neither, do they, Ms. Kirtridge?" he said, peering at me carefully. "You and your brother and your father."

I felt the semblance of a smile evaporate. He was testing me, maybe trying to see how far he could push me before I broke down and unraveled the fake story I had told him before.

"Yeah," I said, putting the shoe back on the wall. *He's on to you. You unblack black girl.* I had already turned and was halfway out of the store when he caught up to me.

"Hey, can't I—can I walk you to your car?" He looked genu-inely concerned, and I wondered if I had misread him.

I looked left and right. There was a short white lady shopping for soccer shorts with her impatient grade-school son. The sales girl was studying her nails behind the cash register. No one was watching, but I still felt naked and exposed. He was too near me and I could smell him, could almost recognize the soap he used, and it clouded my thoughts and even stifled my fear for an instant and I said, somehow, yes, and he smiled again and there was nothing else to do but fall in beside him as we walked through the mall and out to my car. By the time we got there, I felt a little grateful that I'd had to park so far from the entrance. True, I'd have to tough out another game in my old Nikes, but the monolith was even more cracked.

PART
Two

CHAPTER SEVENTEEN

"You seem different," Kit said, while we washed the dishes. It was my turn to clean the pots and pans for the week, but she had magically appeared beside me in the kitchen, brandishing a steel wool scrubber when I was halfway through.

I looked at her sideways. "Different like how?"

She laughed. "I don't know. *Different.* Happier."

I felt my face color, and I focused on scraping charred bacon grease from the bottom of the frying pan. *There is no way I'm telling you. You don't have access to every-damn-thing.*

"Happy is good, though," she said, throwing some suds at my eye.

• • •

In truth, there wasn't much to tell that Kit would have cared about. Reggie and I had talked mainly about baseball during the five minutes it took to walk to my car and the ten minutes we spent sitting on my hood before I finally opened my door and got in. He seemed to sense I was most comfortable when things were between the foul lines.

I met Reggie again the next week to see a movie, and three days later, we met at his favorite Japanese restaurant for tempura, which I had never tried.

"That ain't right," he said, when he found that out. "What do you eat at your house, anyway? Oh yeah, you elite baseball heads probably eat no fried foods at all, huh?"

I shrugged. "French fries sometimes."

He snickered. "Shit. Your dad counts them too, I bet."

I had mentioned almost nothing about my family to him and hoped to keep it that way. We had already tacitly agreed to just drop the incident at the pizzeria; it was like we both viewed it as an anomaly—a hole I had mistakenly fallen into when I wasn't looking.

"So what's he like, your dad?" he asked, dipping fried shrimp into sauce. "He's like a legend in this town. Must be weird."

"Not really," I said. "He's just like everybody else. There's nothing to tell."

Reggie bit off half of the shrimp. "For real?" he asked, peering at me incredulously.

"Yup," I said. I chewed on some rice and tried to look as nonchalant as possible. I couldn't really believe I was eating dinner with a *black person*. And not just any black person, but *a hot black guy who might be interested in me*. What he wanted from me, however, I could not fathom. I had a theory that it had less to do with me and more to do with Dad.

Reggie shook his head. "You're a strange bird, Alex Kirtridge," he said. "Definitely not like anybody else."

I scanned his face, to see if he was making fun of me. Mirth certainly played at the edges of his mouth, but there was nothing malicious or mean there. It was more like he got a kick out of me. I wondered what he would say to any of his black friends about me, if he ever talked with them about it. Would he tell them I was mixed and laugh with them about how my hair was too frizzy?? Did he compare the way I said "No," to the way they said, "Hell naw," and conclude it was because I was too white?

. . .

A few days later, Reggie and I ran in Bayard Park and then got breakfast at Bruegger's Bagels. Running was training for baseball, so technically this too was between the foul lines. These were the spaces where I always felt most comfortable, most in my own skin. But then Reggie asked when he could meet my family.

"My family?" I asked as we ran through a small stand of trees. Maybe it was Dad that he really wanted to get to know. That had happened to me before, but it had been years.

"Yeah, you know—your mom, dad, Jason and your sister," said Reggie. "What's her name again?"

"Kit," I said, pumping my arms harder.

"Yeah," he said. "All of them. It would be great to meet them. My mom always says you don't really know a person till you meet their family."

I could see a trickle of sweat slowly making its way down his forehead.

Reggie's mother, a paralegal at the district attorney's office, had taken us to lunch the week before. Not once during the entire conversation did she say anything that let me know why she thought Reggie was hanging out with me. Were we friends? Something more?

"Let me think about it," I said. I hoped he would see I was uncomfortable with the idea and then just drop it. But that wasn't what happened at all.

We were half a mile from the end of the trail, but Reggie just stopped right there. "I don't feel like running anymore. Got things to do at home." His tone was clipped and agitated.

He was about to turn around when I grabbed his arm. "Reg—what's wrong?" I could feel the angry bulge in his bicep.

When he faced me, his beautiful, kind eyes flashed with anger—something I'd never seen before.

"Not once in the weeks we been together do you ever talk about introducing me to anyone. Not once do you even talk about your family and friends to me. Now . . . I don't know if this is about you being embarrassed of me or what, but I want to know what the problem is."

My eyes were about to pop out of their sockets. I couldn't help it; I started to laugh. "Me embarrassed of *you*?"

"What's so goddamn funny?" he asked, staring me down. He was pissed.

"I'm sorry—I just . . . The thought of me being embarrassed of you is just so ridiculous that I just couldn't even believe you could think that."

"What am I supposed to think?" he asked, wiping the sweat from his brow.

I looked down the trail, at another couple jogging together—were Reggie and I a couple? They looked forty-ish and exhausted. Perhaps they had had this conversation years ago and had dealt with it so appropriately that they could now enjoy long runs together on Sunday morning without incident. But there was Reggie, in front of me, tired and sweaty. I had to answer him. I had to say something. "I didn't want to bring this up, but it's . . . my dad." I bit my lower lip. Why was lying to him so easy? "He kind of freaks out about me and guys. I just . . . haven't wanted to deal with it."

Reggie studied me, deciding whether or not to believe me. Deciding whether or not I was worth his time. "Is that the truth, Alex?" he asked. He stepped closer. "Because sometimes I get the feeling that you're not telling me the whole truth."

I hiccupped and stepped away from him. He was black and my family was white; he wouldn't want me if he saw how much of that whiteness—the speech, the walk, the attitude—had become ingrained in me. Just seeing me alone like this, without them to compare me to, he could really believe that I was "my own person," as he often told me. But stacking me up against my family, he would come to quite a different conclusion.

"It's the truth," I said softly.

Reggie took a long sip from his water bottle and then sighed. He stared at a birch tree beside us, thinking. I hiccupped again, and finally he said, "Okay. We can work around that."

I nodded, and then we started running again, in silence. But my mind was screaming in my skull: *You're just like him. A fucking liar.*

• • •

"So why did they adopt you?" Reggie asked the next night as he stirred vegetables in a wok. His mom had worked nights since he was little, so Reggie was quite used to cooking himself dinner. And I had gotten quite used to lying to my parents every time I saw Reggie. I wondered if Jason noticed I was doing stuff with "friends" a lot more. "I don't get it—they were able to have Jason and Kit."

I swallowed the lump in my throat. "They couldn't get pregnant, so they adopted me. Then, right after all the papers went through, my mom got pregnant with Jason. He was a minor miracle, apparently, like Kit."

"For real?" Reggie asked, turning down the heat. "That's some shit."

I tapped my heels against the wooden stool I was perched on. "My mom used to say that she was always scared to meet with the people from the adoption agency right before they got me, because she was worried they wouldn't give me to them if they knew she was pregnant." It was weird saying all this stuff out loud. They were stories I had known since I was little, but I had never told them to anyone.

Reggie shook his head. "They'd do that? They'd give you to someone else?"

I shrugged. "Probably not. My mom is prone to exaggeration." Reggie's dog nudged my knee. I bent down to pet him, trying to think of something else to talk about. But Reggie beat me to it.

"Must be strange being the only black person in the family," he said.

There it was again, that word *black*. But it sounded so different coming out of Reggie's mouth than Dad's. When he said it, it was like he meant we were part of one big family—and a strong one, too.

"Yeah," I said. "It's . . . weird." I felt a strange sense of loneliness wash over me.

Reggie pushed the vegetables onto the steaming rice in front of him. "This stuff's ready. Want to help me bring it to the table?"

"Yeah," I said, and walked toward him. I grabbed the plates, and suddenly his arms were around me and he was kissing my neck. His lips felt soft on my skin—not at all how I had imagined. The plates were wobbling in my hands. I put them down. He turned me around and kissed my chin, my nose, my forehead, and finally my lips.

"The fine Ms. Kirtridge," he said, pulling away from me. "Been wanting to do that all day."

Once again, I resisted the urge to laugh. "Really?" I asked, trying to savor the sensation of my first kiss. I wanted my lips to remember.

He looked at me incredulously. "You don't know?"

I looked down at the floor.

Reggie ran his fingers down my right arm, making my hair stand up. This was the arm that fielded catches, that swung the bat with power and precision. "*Fine* is definitely the word. *And* smart, *and* a kick-ass ball player," he said in my ear. "Naw, you ain't like them other girls."

I laughed and leaned into him, the first boy I had touched, the first black person who had wanted me. He held me in a hug like that for a few minutes, while our food got cold. I thought about my birth father then and wondered if he had held my mother this way, if they had talked about having me, or if it had just happened.

Reggie's grandmom was at her weekly card game, but his

mother came home not long after that, so things didn't progress much beyond that kiss. But not because I wasn't interested.

"Girl, you reaping the benefits of my home-training now," Mrs. Carter said to me, as she picked up a sautéed vegetable from Reggie's overflowing wok. "You know how many men I woulda shacked up with if they just knew how to cook some damn rice?"

She and Reggie cracked up. It was cool looking at each of them, seeing the obvious closeness and affection, the way they just "got" each other. And the language they used with each other made me feel a comfortable kind of warm, but also nervous, like I would soon be asked to participate in something I admired but could not produce. Black English, I was just beginning to see, often had that effect on me. It was beautiful, but so foreign, and a liability around black people. Once it began, I became filled with fear that it would reveal the whiteness that was not just on the outside.

"Ma, stop playin'," said Reggie. "Dad knew how to cook rice, and some legendary barbecue, greens—the whole nine. But it still didn't stop you from throwing his ass out on the doorstep."

I could not imagine anyone in my family swearing at the dinner table, much less talking about a family breakup in this way. Under the table, I squeezed my fingers together and felt the usual hiccups forming in my windpipe.

Mrs. Carter snorted. "No, you right. You right," she said, waving a half-eaten carrot slice at Reggie. "Niggers don't know how to act right, they get they ass on the curb. No matter how good they greens is."

My fork fell on the table, and the sound made me jump. If I was embarrassed at my reaction, I need not have worried because the two of them completely collapsed in laughter after this outburst, snorting and falling over each other on the table. I was the last thing on their minds. "I have to use the bathroom," I said, almost whispered really, as I stood up.

They nodded, and Mrs. Carter pointed behind me. "Down the hall to the right, honey."

I pushed out my seat too fast, and almost ran away from the table. The house was a modest ranch with what looked like two bedrooms. Reggie's bedroom was about the size of the walk-in closet in my parents' master bedroom, and his door was bent at an odd angle, and wouldn't really shut. Since there was only one other room, Reggie's mom and grandmom must have shared it. I grimaced a little, thinking of being a grown, professional, and self-possessed woman like his mother and having to share such a small, personal space with your mother. I wondered how they did it—not like they had much of a choice. With Reggie's dad gone, his mom had to be the only bread-winner in the family. I was sure that this house in this run-down neighborhood was what they could afford. And it was funny because I would have been embarrassed of the peeling paint on the walls, the dirty vinyl flooring that obviously hadn't been changed in years, the pockmarked and broken molding everywhere. But they didn't seem to notice it, or maybe just didn't care. This was a world apart from my house, where the whole house had to be cleaned, everything in its proper place and spotless before any "outsiders" (and for my parents this included friends and even extended family) could be let in.

Worn pictures of Reggie playing baseball in elementary and middle school hung in cheap frames at awkward angles on the hall-way walls. He was even cuter as a kid, I thought to myself as I hurried to the bathroom. With a big dimple in his right cheek and bright bursting eyes he must have been a favorite of the girls since kinder-garten. I turned to the right and faced a door with a large wooden placard with "Family Makes a Home" plastered across it in cursive with long wildflower stems winding through each letter. I stifled a laugh and pushed open the door. The bathroom was perhaps the tiniest I'd ever seen, with an aging toilet and sink almost mashed together on the other side of the room. I put my hand over my mouth and nose as a sickly rose scent flooded my senses. It was like being in Grandma Kirtridge's bathroom—everything was spotless but almost funereal. I opened the door quickly and sat down on the toilet before I had time to follow this line of thought further. The truth was that I liked the Carters; really liked them, in fact. And I felt guilty for judging them. They had never been anything but nice to me. But at the same time, there was a part of me that couldn't turn it off.

Looking up at the cracked ceiling, I began to hiccup, and I cursed each one as it left my mouth. This was what always happened when I got too nervous, or when my anxiety got the better of me. *This is all there is*, said the voice in my head, the same voice that had said it for years, mostly lying in bed in the dead of night while the rest my family slept, but also occasionally in moments like this. Moments in daily life that felt out of whack for some reason I couldn't pinpoint. *This is all there is, and this is all there will ever be*, the voice said again, louder. I knew in a moment it would be screaming in my ears if I couldn't get control of myself. I balled my hands into fists and rested them on my forehead, rocking. *No, this can't be it. There has to be something more.*

I willed myself to think of something different, something concrete, in order to distract myself. Images of baseball games and laying out for fly balls came into my head, but they were fleeting. Instead, what came to mind was sledding on the huge hill at McKnight Park, sixth grade, two black kids from another school snickering at me, *We ain't got all day!* while I fiddled with my sled in line at the top of the hill. *Make it snappy, nappy!* They and some white kids laughing at me and my disheveled hair. My stomach churning, my face coloring. Now more hiccups coming. *This is all there will ever be.* I rocked my collapsed legs back and forth on the toilet lid, and pressed my palms into my eyes, pushing my brain to envision something—anything—else.

You a real mess, you know that? You muthafucking Oreo wanna-be white girl. A brash mass of black bodies huddled in hallway corners at West High, always somehow finding me, even when I did my best to blend in and avoid them. They always found me. *What the hell is going on with your hair, anyway?* A hand pulling one of my curls. My head yanked back, then snapping forward. The endless search for words, a rebuttal, anything to make them leave me alone. Nothing coming. Just my legs moving me along as fast as possible, to get away from that blackness that would engulf me otherwise—and then what would I be? *I'm not black anyway*, my mind would scream, but the phrase would never make its way to my mouth. *I'm mixed.* Dad's answer. I hiccupped now, disappointed that that was still all I had on them. *And at least I'll be going to college, unlike you idiots.*

I bowed my head in shame and tried to come back to the present—even if it was a present in which I realized that Reggie would never want me if he knew how the black kids really saw me, and how I saw myself. The truth was, I wasn't black at all. Not by objective assessment, and certainly not by choice. I opened my eyes again and looked up at the ceiling, counting the cracks that radiated from the dingy fluorescent fixture. When I got up to fourteen, the hiccups had almost subsided. Then a knock at the door.

"Alex, you okay in there?" Mrs. Carter's voice was warm with concern on the other side of the door. "You just been in there a minute, so I thought I'd check."

I thrust my feet down to the ground—probably a little too forcefully—and tried to make my voice as level as possible. "I'm fine, Mrs. Carter. Sorry. Almost done in here." I stood up and turned on the sink, letting the water fall into the drain as my dry hands gripped the basin.

"No problem at all," she said. "Take as long as you need." She sounded a little embarrassed now. "I was just checking."

I opened the door abruptly and faced her. She wore a simple blazer and matching beige skirt, her hair straight but curled inwards at the ends. She had given Reggie her bright eyes, which I suspected and feared could see as much as his could.

"All set," I said, stepping toward her. "Let's eat."

She put her hand on my back and lightly directed me toward the kitchen table.

CHAPTER EIGHTEEN

In 2009, when I was ten and Jason was nine, Hank Aaron came up to Madison to scout out some local talent and visit friends. At the time, Hank was director of player development for the Brewers and was always traveling somewhere to look at a prospect. Dad had somehow convinced Hank's personal assistant that it would be worth his time to stop by batting practice of the number-three-ranked Little League team in the country that afternoon, since he would be in the area anyway.

At 3:35, twenty of us were hot, sweaty, and ready for a water break. We had been swinging at pitches with all our might on the off chance that Hank Aaron would walk in at the exact moment we were up and see us slam one out of the park.

"Alex, you're up," Dad said, from behind the cage.

I sighed; my right wrist ached from snapping it so hard during all the previous at bats. I knew better than to mention this to Dad, however.

"This sucks," Jason whispered in my ear.

I wiped my dirty hand across my forehead, which ended up only making my sweat dirty as it dripped into my eyes.

Logan, my teammate then and now, is this pasty, pale-faced white boy who was thin as a rail then. He could throw anything and everything at any speed, and at any location, even the pitches that weren't allowed in the league for our age group (like curve balls). It hurt my head to swing against him in the middle of the afternoon like this; I had to think too much, and my temple was already throbbing.

He hid his face from me behind the mitt. I sighed, lifting my bat higher over my right shoulder. The sun felt like it was burning a hole in my skull. He went through the windup and then delivered. All of it happened so fast that I barely had time to think, and then the ball was in the catcher's mitt, and I was still standing there, waiting, staring into the sky.

"You can't wait for the pitcher to make up his mind. You have make up yours," a deep voice said behind me. I turned around and found myself face to face with Hank Aaron. He was wearing an old Brewer's cap that was torn along the brim, a T-shirt, and light-weight khaki pants. His smile was broad and sincere, and it paralyzed me.

"You just let him dictate the terms of the at bat, and you can never afford to do that," he told me. "I'm not going to talk to you about where your hips should be, or the right way to hold the bat. I leave the mechanics to other people, who know better."

Dad snorted. He knew, like we did, that there was no one who knew better than Hank Aaron.

Aaron leaned forward, so that he could look me straight in the eyes. "All you need to know is what kind of pitch he's likely to throw, what his release point will be, its location, and the speed." He laughed. "That sounds like a lot, I know, but all I'm really saying is study him. He's on your own team, right?"

I nodded, though what I really wanted to do was reach out and touch his hand. *That's Hank Aaron's hand.*

"So, you know him, and what he's likely to throw," he said.

I nodded again. Then I looked out at Logan, still perched on the mound, watching all of us in confusion. I felt sorry for him, out there all by himself.

"He throws me lots of fastballs," I said. "High and inside."

Hank Aaron stood up and crossed his arms over his chest.

I cleared my throat. "I think he likes to throw one fast, to get me swinging, and then he tends to make the next ones off-speed."

Hank Aaron nodded. "Because he's a good pitcher. But even good pitchers have to give up a few hits when they face good hitters."

"Yeah," I said. He had a face that made me want to tell him everything: how I was the only girl on the team, how I was Jason's sister and Dad's daughter, and how I was going up to the show someday.

"Try again," he said, gently. "Think about what's next, where it will be, and when." Then he stepped away from the plate and walked behind the cage.

I took a deep breath and looked for Jason in the group of teammates gathered beside the cage. I finally found his Derek Jeter T-shirt and ecstatic grin. He gave me the thumbs-up and winked. I tried to smile, but the sides of my mouth would not move. I didn't even want to look at Dad. I turned my attention back to the plate and dug my feet deep into the dirt.

Logan went into his windup and then released the ball when it was well over his shoulder. I anticipated, swung, and connected, pulling the ball toward third base. I dropped the bat and began to run toward first, Hank Aaron's eyes on my back pushing me forward.

A few strides into my run, the first baseman's face appeared before me, red and blurry. "Foul ball!" he yelled, and my chest tightened. Hank Aaron had told me how to hit it, and I hadn't listened well enough, because the ball hadn't stayed between the foul lines. I stopped running and turned around. I didn't want to look at

Dad, Jason, or Hank Aaron, so I deliberately stared at my cleats on the long walk back to the cage.

"You did good, Alex," Hank Aaron said as I finally reached him. There was nothing sarcastic about his tone; he was telling me the truth. "I hope you don't mind, your brother told me your name," he said, his arm around Jason, who looked like he might implode from all the excitement.

"That's a good start, a real good start," Hank Aaron continued. "You just need to work some to perfect your swing a little, so that you swing just a little earlier on a pitch like that. But the important thing is that you're making up your mind to hit on him," he said. "Once you do that, it's only a matter of time."

My face was starting to burn: Hank Aaron thought that it was only a matter of time before I would become a great hitter. Hank Aaron had instructed me, Alexandra Lynn Kirtridge, and I had begun to learn.

"But you know, that ball almost didn't roll foul, though, third baseman," he shouted up the field. "And you really weren't in the correct position to field it in case it was fair. You need to position yourself on the field according to each hitter. For Alex, I'd say you probably need to move in and to the left a bit, so you can be in prime position to field the ball and then throw to first for the out. Here, I'll show you. Let me play third for a minute. Alex, you go back to the plate and hit again. I'll show you what I mean."

Dad threw him a mitt, and he jogged toward third.

Jason and I locked eyes. We were going to play with Hank Aaron, who hit 755 home runs and had 6,856 bases. Hank Aaron, the all-time leader in total bases and runs batted in.

"Mr. Aaron!" a high-pitched female voice yelled onto the field. I whipped around to see who it belonged to and spotted a thin, white woman, dressed in a light blue business suit, in the stands. "I'm sorry, but we may have to cut this short. We're already going to be late for your four thirty."

My stomach sank; there was a certain kind of authority to her tone that would be hard for anyone, even Hank Aaron, to ignore. I knew that he would be leaving us.

Hank Aaron paused in mid-stride, considering her words. A minute ago, he had been smiling, but now his face was serious, almost inaccessible. "I forgot about that," he said. He laughed. "Guess I was having too much fun out here with you guys." He started walking toward the stands. "Just have too many appointments in one day."

We almost played ball with Hank Aaron. We were ready to pull the long ball.

He was shaking Dad's hand, thanking him for the opportunity to meet each of us. "They're a great group, I can see why you've gone so far with them," he said. "I'll be watching for them, especially that little girl. She's got something. Smarts and tenacity."

Dad's face was positively glowing. He thanked Hank Aaron for taking the time out of his busy schedule to work with us.

Tenacity. It was a strange and awkward-sounding word, and I had no idea what it meant, though I could tell from the way Hank Aaron said it that it was a good thing.

He turned and waved to us one last time before he disappeared into the darkness of the stadium corridor.

"Goodbye, Hank Aaron," I said under my breath. It seemed like he was gone right after he arrived.

CHAPTER NINETEEN

At some level, I knew this was going to happen—I was a likely valedictorian, not a moron. But it still caught me by surprise.

.285/.355/.399. A slash line in decline was what I was. Two weeks before the state tournament, I found myself in an extended batting slump. Dad now had me batting seventh—or worse, he'd taken to keeping me out of the starting lineup "to rest" and then pinch running me—if we had a lead. And that wasn't all, either. These strange, ever-moving blobs on my chest were growing bigger by the day and making things tight everywhere. Lying in bed at night, I could almost feel my hips starting to spread, and my sense of balance was off at the plate. I knew that things could change rapidly in my body, but I had no idea it would happen so fast. Meanwhile, Jason's hands were growing, his knuckles bulbous and pink—like Dad's. When he talked, he stretched out his fingers and moved them around in circles, which was something I had never seen him do before; that was how Dad talked. My hands were still small, my fingers stubby. They weren't growing, and when I talked I moved them a little, but they mostly remained still, controlled, at my side.

Jason and Dad pretended not to notice what was going on. At dinner or on their way to a game, they made extra efforts to include me in discussion and strategizing. And they would both compliment me excessively when I got a hit or made a great play, things they would not have even mentioned back when I was playing well.

But I wasn't going to give up so easily. Early mornings after running, I spent hours in front of the mirror in my room. I knew a lot of girls at school who carefully monitored everything they ate, mortified that they might add an extra pound to their hips or ass. But that wasn't my problem; if anything, I would have welcomed the extra weight on my frame. Next to the guys, I looked like I might blow away in the wind. I would turn my arms back and forth in front of the mirror, analyzing the flex of a bicep, wishing it thicker. The guys were all developing six-packs on their stomachs, but a small mound of flesh remained stubbornly attached to my abdomen no matter how many sit-ups I did. My thighs were, perhaps, my biggest disappointment: they were as malleable as Play-Doh. Dad had always told us that strong legs were what really generated power, so all of us were constantly striving to shape them. Jason adopted a strict exercise, weight, and diet regimen, which was yielding incredible results. No such luck for me.

This can't be it. That was the thought that usually visited me those mornings, in front of the mirror. *There has to be something I can do.* I vowed to improve somehow, improve to the point where Dad would know he was a fool to ever doubt who I was and what I was capable of. There was no good reason why it couldn't be done; I just had to focus. *Focus. Focus.* I began running twice as far as everyone else. I lifted less weight than the guys but did more reps and sets. I strictly monitored everything I consumed. Sweets and fried foods were the first things to go, followed by salty snacks with saturated fat and high carbohydrate content. One night

Reggie cooked me a high-protein tofu and organic vegetable stir-fry, adamant that it would slowly but inevitably build my stamina and muscle.

But a few days into the regimen, my body let me down again. We were up four in the seventh during the regional championship game when Dad had me pinch run. The batter had failed to move me over, but Dad kept me in at center. I knew that this was my chance to show him and everybody that I was still the old Alex, the best player on the field, who wasn't scared of anything and who was going to be the first girl to make it.

As he headed toward number 715, it had become more and more difficult for Hank, I remembered. *Dear Nigger, You black animal, I hope you never live long enough to hit more home runs than the great Babe Ruth.* The hate mail had increased as he approached the record, but he put it back somewhere outside of his sight. Somewhere he couldn't see it every time he had come up to bat.

The umpire signaled the end of a time-out, and the batter stepped up to the plate. I licked my lips; they were as dry and cracked as my throat. I looked over at the guys on the bench, who were trading sips from a bright green water bottle. A streak of silver on the water bottle threw the bright sunlight back in my eyes and I winced. It suddenly felt like I hadn't had a drink in a very, very long time. The batter took his stance, and I crouched down. *Focus. Focus.* I wanted him to drive it straight into center field, maybe a bit to my right so that I would have to run and then make a sliding catch. Something dramatic. Our pitcher stretched and delivered. My eyes fixed on the ball as it left his hand. It was like it was carving a tunnel through the air, turning it violet and yellow and light blue as it shattered into pieces. I was conscious that I was waiting for the pieces to come back together, and then I was conscious that my eyes were actually shut, not open. What I was watching was occurring in a different world, on a different plane. I was here, but I was not here. I was lying in the grass, my feet buckled beneath me, arms splayed out at my sides.

"Alex! Alex!" a voice said anxiously in my ear. It was Hank Aaron, my true father. It was my birth father, Keith.

"Is she all right?" said another voice.

A hand on my face. Someone pouring water on my forehead.

"Oh, God. Oh, God." That was Jason. That was my brother. I opened my eyes.

"What happened?" I asked.

His eyes were deep with worry, his skin almost ghostly. He took my hand.

"Are you all right?" said Dad. He was crouched down beside me. "Can you see okay?"

I concentrated on the endless blades of grass that surrounded us. "I can see fine." I sat up slowly and rubbed my head. "What happened?"

"It looked like you fainted," said Jason. "You just fell."

I frowned. I didn't believe him. I pushed my palms into the grass and shoved myself up to my feet.

"Whoa!" said Dad. "Stay put. They're bringing a stretcher."

I laughed, already starting toward my glove, about a foot away in the grass. "I'm fine, Dad."

Dad and Jason exchanged glances.

"Alex," Dad said. "I—I'm sorry, but you're done for the day." There was no mistaking the regret in his voice. It made me angry.

"I'm fine," I said.

He sighed. He looked at the ground, then back up at me. "Alex, you fainted. You're going to go drink some water, and then you're done for the day."

I winced at the finality of his tone. There would be no amazing plays made today; I would end the game having barely played two minutes of it. I wouldn't even appear on the score card. I picked up my mitt and began to walk silently back to the dugout. All the guys on the field clapped as I passed them. I wanted to flip them off.

Walking beside me, Dad said, "You definitely need to rethink that whole diet you're on. I think it's doing you more harm than good."

● ● ●

I lay in bed that night, dressed in tattered shorts and an old state champs T-shirt. Dad and I hadn't spoken since I left the field. Jason had tried to strike up a conversation a couple times, but eventually he let me disappear, too.

"It's going to be okay, honey," Mom had told me a few minutes after I got in bed. She rubbed my back like she always did when I was younger, to calm me. "I'm sure your dad has a plan."

Mom had patted me on the forehead, and then left me there in the darkness of my room, shadows looming large in corners, lights from the neighborhood bouncing off the walls. The rough sheets against my skin reassured me a little, let me know that I was still alive, that I was still here, barely.

Our house was big, but it was old, with wooden floors and echoing plaster walls. If the house was quiet, I could often hear conversations—even hushed ones—in the living room. And the house was definitely quiet tonight.

"You knew that this day would come," I heard Mom say.

I stepped out of bed, tiptoeing toward the doorway.

"We just . . . We need to wait and see. She might still pull out of it," Dad said.

I disappeared into the dark hallway and crept toward the railing so I could hear better.

"Terry . . . We just all need to be prepared. Because she might not."

My stomach sank.

Dad's voice rose. "I've always been prepared. Softball is always an option."

I put my hand over my mouth to stifle a gasp.

"You just have to keep your ace in the hole as long as you can possibly play it."

"You turned your ace in a long time ago, and you've made other things work. You thought you could play forever, too." Mom sighed. "She's going through so much right now, I guess we really shouldn't be surprised."

"You hold out as long as you can and then you have no choice. But Alex is different. She never gives in."

CHAPTER
TWENTY

No one talked about my fainting spell, but I saw them watching me more carefully now than ever before. If I tripped, there was always an arm to catch me. If I wiped the sweat off my brow, at least two people handed me water bottles. I tried to smile about it all, but what I really felt like doing was smacking all the hands, all the help, away.

After practice two days after I fainted, I came out of the locker room wearing my warm-up gear, my sports bag slung over one shoulder, to find Dad huddled with Kyle, who played some right field and backed up Jason at first. Dad was waving his hands around, pointing alternately to Kyle and then to right, left, and center fields. Kyle kept on glancing at the field, looking back at Dad attentively, and then nodding. I couldn't hear anything, but I knew exactly what he was telling him—*your job as center fielder is to read the whole field, not just field the center.* He had told me so many times. I turned around and walked around the corner, out of sight. Dad was doing the smart thing, I knew, by getting Kyle ready. *There are teams that win and then there are individuals. But in my game, you have to be both.*

My disappearance from the starting nine was about to be permanent.

• • •

At least there was one thing that I was still good at—running distance; my hips hadn't thrown that off. After I got through the pain of the first five or ten minutes and acclimated my body to what it felt like to work that hard, it was almost like I was in another world. Time slowed down, and everything around me blurred into one big backdrop. Even my thoughts slowed down. *Breathe. Turn right. Breathe. Just a little further.* My stomach tightened. *Breathe. You can do this.* I was strong while I was running because there was never anything else to conquer but the next step.

Which was why I wasn't so surprised to find myself in front of Reggie's house one evening a couple of days after I'd seen Dad with Kyle. All I was doing was running; not thinking, just moving, but somehow I ended up at 5498 Juniper Lane. His house wasn't close to mine—a little over six miles away, so in some part of my brain I must have been thinking about going there all along.

I paced in front of the house for a good three minutes, breathing heavily, trying to decide what to do. I was drenched in sweat, and my hair was frizzing like it always did when I pulled it back into a tight ponytail for a workout. It wasn't exactly the look I wanted to present to Reggie. I bit off a hangnail. Still, I wanted to see him. He'd been busy with his job stocking products at Home Depot, and I'd been all baseball, so our relationship, whatever it was, had dwindled to texts in the last week.

I stomped up the stairs to the door and willed myself to knock. I didn't even have time to resent my decision when the door flew open and an elderly black woman half my size, half hunched over, and dressed in a bright pink dress and low white heels stood before me. She had short, waxy, straightened hair that didn't entirely cover her head, and what looked like fake pearl earrings clipped on. This had to be Reggie's grandma. I was just working on a smile when she asked if she could help me. I smelled meat cooking—pork, I guessed—and also fried potatoes. My stomach rumbled, and I felt air beginning to stick in my windpipe, the telltale signs of the hiccups that would follow. I blinked. The woman smiled. "You okay?" she asked. I tried to smile and nodded, but still no sound came out.

"Grandmom, who's that?" I heard from behind her. Then footsteps, then Reggie's face—long, feminine eyelashes and baby cheeks. "Alex," he said.

"Yeah," I coughed out. The last time we had spoken was a few days before. I'd had to get off the phone for dinner and told him I would call him back but never did. Just a few texts. Nothing special.

"How'd . . ." He looked behind me, scanning for a car, I guess. "You bike?"

I shook my head. "Ran."

"Right," said Reggie, taking in my slightly matted hair and glistening arms and legs.

Across the street, the kids were barking out orders to each other about some kind of tag game they were playing. A TV screen blared in the room to the right of where Reggie and his grandma stood. It sounded like *American Idol*.

"I'm Rebecca," the woman said suddenly, extending her hand. "Reggie's grandmom. You must be his girl."

He mentioned me to his grandma, even? I felt my face grow hot.

"Momma, who's at the door?" Mrs. Carter called from the kitchen.

"It's just Alex, Ma," Reggie called back.

"Oh, Alex! Haven't seen that girl in a minute. Tell her to come in and have some dinner with us."

I stepped backward, almost tipping on the edge of the step. "Oh no," I said. "I didn't mean to interrupt. I just was over here and I thought . . ."

"Girl, come on in and eat some food with us already. Everything's getting cold," said Reggie's grandma. Then she leaned into me, screwing her face into a tight little ball.

I tried to smile but could feel it wasn't coming. "Oh no, I couldn't . . ." I stammered. Even though I had eaten with Reggie plenty of times, and that one time with his mom, too, there was something about this old woman that made me uneasy. Her eyes were not large, but they were bright like Reggie's and Mrs. Carter's, and they looked much more penetrating. Like they had seen plenty in their time, and would have no problem seeing through me. *She'll see it, and know it. The whiteness.*

Reggie's grandma frowned then, sensing my discomfort I think, and crossed her arms across her chest. "If you ain't hungry, you should know better than to disturb folks at this hour. Plain as day that it's dinnertime and folks is eating." She turned around and started shuffling back to the kitchen, mumbling the whole time.

I hiccupped, and before I knew it, tears came to my eyes. Back home, Dad and Mom and Jason and Kit were sitting down to dinner themselves. They would be wondering why my run was taking so long, and they would save me a plate. Even though they knew less about me every day, what they knew was still enough most of the time. And no one, none of them, would ever *try* to make me cry.

"Sorry," I said. Then I turned and ran down the stairs before Reggie or anyone else could see any of the tears fall. There was nothing I hated more than crying in public.

But he ran after me. I heard him shout to his mom that he would be right back, and then the door slam behind him. "Alex!" he yelled, but my legs were moving again and I didn't want them to stop. I brought my arms up and started pumping, and I felt like I was flying, like no one and nothing could stop me from just moving. And then he got a hold of my arm.

"Alex, wait!" he said again, and I snapped back into him. "What . . ." he said, calmer now. "What's going on?"

I didn't want to look up. I didn't want him to see. I hiccupped. The kids across the street were finally beginning their tag game, screaming and laughing at each other.

Reggie leaned down and tried to see my face, but I turned away.

He sighed. "You're not mad at my grandmom, are you? She's just . . . on a different level than the rest of us. She's too old to put up with being polite now. Truth be told, I hear she wasn't that keen on the whole concept back in the day, anyway. But she didn't mean anything by what she said to you, I hope you know. She really just wanted you to come in and break bread with us, you know?"

There was a fly buzzing around my head and I wanted to smack it, but it was moving too fast.

"Alex?" he asked, and I looked up, finally. His eyelashes were even longer up close. And there was this one line across his forehead that was getting deeper with each moment I didn't respond. So I decided to say something—anything.

"There is no way I can keep on playing baseball. And I don't know what else to do." The tears were blinding my vision, they were coming so fast. Reggie put his arm around me and squeezed my shoulders. I just wanted to leave, but at the same time, I couldn't stop talking. "You're the only person I even talk to who's black, and I'm black. Don't you think that's a little fucked up?" I said, wiping away the tears with the back of my hand.

His brow furrowed.

The words were pouring out; I didn't know where they were coming from. "My parents can't even admit that I'm black anyway. My dad's like, 'Oh, she's just half black.' Such a crock of shit." I was walking faster by the minute, the intensity of my steps scaring the kids and adults who passed us onto the street or yard. We were already almost to the end of his block.

"But aren't you?" Reggie asked.

I peered at him. He was asking for real. "Aren't I what?"

"Aren't you half black?"

I laughed. "Yeah. So?"

He shrugged. "So, maybe it's like he's just stating it like it's a fact or something. You know, because he doesn't know what else to do."

I suddenly found myself shouting at him. "He's my fucking father and he doesn't know what to do with me?"

Reggie held up his hands. "Whoa, whoa."

A middle-aged woman walking her poodle across the street glared at me. I bet she had known Reggie since he was three or something.

Breathe in. Breathe out. I closed my eyes. "You don't know what it's like to wake up every morning and not know if your skin is really your skin. You don't know how it feels to look like a whole group of people who you've never even fucking spoken to, much less feel a part of. You don't go to West High, you don't even hear half the stuff . . ." I was walking away from him, slowly, and the tears were falling again, hot on my cheeks, hot in my throat and mouth. I didn't even try to brush them away this time. "Yes, I'm a white black girl, okay? Are you happy?" I squeezed my eyes closed, willing all of it, everything I had said and not said, everything that I wanted to be, to go away. *This is all there is.* I inhaled, slowly, and suddenly there were arms around me.

He didn't say anything; he just held me while I cried. It seemed like all the water I had in my body was coming out of my eyes—I cried for a good fifteen minutes. When I felt completely dry and almost empty inside, I wiped my face clean. He took my hand and led me back to his house, around the front to the back door, which he opened slowly and carefully, gesturing for me to come inside.

I hesitated. "They're not here," he said, flipping on a hall light. "They go out and play Spades once a week. I bet they took dinner with them to share with their girls."

I followed him to his bedroom, where he sat me down on his bed, took off my shoes, and laid me down on top of the covers. Then he turned out the lights and stretched out beside me. I wanted to thank him, because I felt my brain finally slowing down, but I was suddenly too tired to speak.

His hands rested on my side for at least an hour. We lay on our hips in an "S" shape, his chest pressing into my back. The clock ticked on, and someone's radio was blasting out on the street. I exhaled deeply when he pushed his hand up under my shirt and onto the small of my back. I had been drifting in and out of sleep, surprised by how comfortable his body felt around me, how easy it was to be with him like this. It was cold in his house—his mother and grandmother liked to pump the air-conditioning in the summer, he said, especially since the heat was hard on his grandmother. So I needed his warmth to heat me.

But when he put his palm on my skin, and then slowly stretched out his fingers, I felt another kind of heat growing in my stomach. He ran his fingers up and down my spine and I shivered.

"You okay?" he whispered in my ear, and I nodded, closing my eyes.

He kissed the nob on the back of my neck, which stuck out so far because I was so skinny. He kissed it so sweetly that I shivered again and turned over to face him.

"What's happening?" I asked.

He looked at me and laughed.

I studied his face to see if I noticed anything new there, anything I hadn't seen before. The only thing I could find were the pores on his nose—I could see each one. I leaned over and kissed them.

I listened to the house. The air conditioner was laboring in the next room and a branch tapped at the windowpane. Someone had finally turned the radio off outside. I couldn't hear any other human sounds, except for us, which calmed me.

He kissed me. This time on the lips. They felt warmer than the rest of him, and I leaned into him. We opened our lips. The heat came again, but this time it had pushed itself down further.

He pressed his body against me, and I felt something stiff push into me. I wanted to laugh.

He pulled back. "What's funny?"

"Nothing," I said.

He looked at me incredulously.

"I'm just . . ." I struggled for the right word. "Nervous." I stroked his arm, and he leaned back on it.

"Yeah," he said. "That's cool." He moved away from me a little, and I immediately felt cold all over again.

I burrowed my head into his chest. "No, that's not what I mean." He stroked my head.

I stared at him. He just looked like he was enjoying touching me, being here, that whatever happened was enough. That made me want to do more with him.

"I want you to touch me," I said.

He smiled and leaned over to kiss the top of my head.

I kissed him on the lips and then slowly pushed my tongue into his mouth. Before I knew what I was doing, my hands were pushing up his shirt. I heard myself moan and blushed. "You are so beautiful," I whispered, and I meant it. His skin was so soft, and my fingertips tripped on the muscles of his torso. I suddenly knew that I had wanted to be with him like this from the moment that we first sat down at the pizzeria. That terrible conversation. Even then, I'd wanted this.

Reggie's hand was traveling back up my back, pushing my sports bra up, over my head.

My breath caught.

He brought his hand back down, further, into my running shorts. "Your ass is just tremendous," he said.

I giggled.

"What?" he said. "I'm just being real with you. It's amazing."

I moved my hand down to his stomach and made circles there. I felt him shiver, and I felt powerful. "What makes an ass 'tremendous?'" I whispered in his ear.

He squeezed it again. "Its shape," he said into my ear. "Its . . . fullness. Trust me when I say that there are few asses in the world that are stacked like this one." He moved his lips up and down my earlobe, nibbling and kissing, and I felt my pelvis grind into him.

My body was mine, and it was not mine. I didn't know what it was doing, and yet it was me.

Late at night in my bed I sometimes touched myself, had even brought myself to orgasm once or twice, but this was so different. For someone else to touch you, to react to you touching them, and to then respond in turn, was compelling in a way I had never experienced before. I knew my right arm could throw an out to first in a second, but I had no idea that it would send shivers through the rest of me if stroked the right way. In some ways, it was like he knew my body better than I did. This was another kind of power, I realized.

Reggie's tongue flicked around my ear, and I moaned and brought him closer to me. We pressed together and he was so hard and his hands were everywhere—I couldn't keep track anymore. When he slid his finger into me, I just held on tight. There was no baseball, there was no Dad, nobody was black and nobody was not black enough, there were just hands and bodies, everything grasping, everything opening.

• • •

I think I slept in the crook of his arm afterward. When I woke up, I texted Kit to tell Mom and Dad that I was on my way back from a long run and would be back within the hour. It wasn't completely a lie, which was why I thought they might believe it—especially if Kit spun it right.

"Gotta go?" Reggie asked, awakened by my movement.

I leaned over and kissed him. "Yeah. They'll be starting to worry."

He nodded and ran his hand over my shoulder.

I shivered and finished tying my shoe. "Thank you," I said, as I stood up. I couldn't quite meet his eyes.

He smiled. "You gonna be okay out there? Running in the night?"

"I do it all the time. Don't worry."

"You," he said, standing up and pulling on his shorts. "I know better than to worry about you. At least out loud."

I laughed. Then we left his bedroom and walked down the hallway to the front door.

"Just text me you're home when you get there," he said, kissing me one more time on the steps. "Not 'cause I'm worried, but you know . . . just 'cause."

I laughed, held up my phone and nodded, taking off at a measured pace under the streetlights. The steady tread of my foot soles on the pavement fell right in line with what I whispered into the hazy summer night, almost all the way home: *Reggie. Reggie. Reggie. Reggie.*

CHAPTER
TWENTY-ONE

Dad and I stood in the backyard a few days later, dusk coming behind us, throwing the ball around. We each took a step back after every throw, and our voices were rising as the exercise went on.

"Waukesha got word that they might have to play us. They're not pleased." He grinned, catching the ball.

The Wisconsin State Baseball Tournament would be held in late June this year, over three days. The top teams from sectionals would battle each other the first day. The winners of those games would advance to the semifinals the next. The two teams left standing in each division would face off on day three for the finals.

"Better us than Eau Claire," I said. Eau Claire had won States three out of the last seven years, although they weren't playing so well this year for some reason.

Dad frowned. "What do you mean? Eau Claire sucks." He threw the ball back, and I watched it spin toward me.

"They don't." I reached out and grabbed the ball. "They suck *right now*, but they might not suck in a couple of weeks. There's a difference."

Dad snorted. I wondered if he knew that we weren't really talking about Eau Claire, but about me. "Eau Claire sucks," he repeated.

I shivered. It would soon be dark. I heaved a high, arcing throw toward Dad.

"They couldn't find their asshole if it bit them in the face right now," said Dad, making a lazy basket catch. "A winning team has to win games. Everything else is just nice stories for the history books. What have they done *lately*?" He skimmed the ball across the grass at me—a not quite hard grounder.

I charged the ball, taking it barehanded a few hops earlier than he probably expected and whipped it back at him sidearm. The ball rocketed toward his head. "Hey!" He had to twist awkwardly to glove the ball. "What are you trying to do, kill me?" He glared at me.

I wasn't grinning. Not quite. "Sorry, Dad."

He looked at me funny from across the yard. Even though he had thrown around with me in this very spot and at the same time of day thousands of times, I got the feeling that in that moment, he wasn't sure he recognized me. And then it passed. "It's okay," he said. "Just be more careful next time."

I punched my glove, nodding. "Sure," I said.

• • •

The next night, Reggie and I sat under an elm tree in the park with branches that twisted and turned in the wind. His arms were around me, and I felt safe again but also anxious.

"You okay?" he asked me, in my ear.

I nodded.

"You're a little quiet."

I didn't say anything, just watched a squirrel dig up acorns in the dirt around us.

"Did you tell anybody? About what happened the other night?" he asked, his voice a little strained.

"No," I said.

He kissed the top of my head. "Me neither."

The wind was swirling in my ears. I remembered his lips on my neck, his hand pushing the small of my back into him, the sound of my breath catching, his fingers inside me.

He pulled at a strand of my hair so that the curl straightened, and then he let it go and it bounced back. Reggie laughed. "You got pretty curls, especially in the back."

I picked up a stick and began digging in the dirt. "I don't like it," I said. "It's too frizzy."

"No one wants the hair they got, no matter what kind it is," he said and then pulled on another curl. "I bet your mom doesn't know what to do with it either."

I laughed and dug deeper. The sky was turning from purple to deep blue.

"I don't really get what ya'll do with your hair, but I know my mom, Grandmom, and my sisters get theirs straightened," said Reggie. He shrugged. "They seem to like it well enough." His sisters were both away at college, so I had never met them, had never seen their hair. He snaked his face around so that he was looking at my profile. "You ever been to a black hairdresser?"

I shook my head, thinking that I just might dig all the way to China.

"Well, maybe you should go, see what you think."

I paused in my digging. "Would you really walk in there with your white mother if you had one?" I asked.

"If I needed to get my hair done I would," he said. So many things were so simple for him.

My face colored. "You think I need to get my hair done?"

He snickered. "Now, don't put that on me. You're the one who said you wanted it less frizzy."

CHAPTER TWENTY-TWO

The lights of Glenda's were a raucous, neon blue that left my eyelids scorched. The sign was in cursive and "Black Hair Designs" was written in print below it. Mom pulled the Jeep into the only free available spot, sandwiched between an ancient pea-green Chevy station wagon and a navy Ford Escort. She had picked me up after work at the Cultural Affairs Office and was still dressed in a khaki pantsuit. Her shoulder-length blonde hair was swept back neatly into a bun, not a strand of it out of place. The whole drive over, all I could think about was why I wasn't given hair like that, why mine had to take so much time and effort to tame, why none of the stylists my mom went to ever seemed to know how to cut it. If I had had hair like Mom's, I could just have brushed it in the mornings, pulled it back, and gotten on with the day. Instead, I had to spend at least fifteen minutes every morning dealing with it, and it still looked too frizzy, no matter what I did.

"Okay, ready?" Mom asked. "I have a good feeling about this; this place looks really professional." I got the sense she was saying this mostly to herself. When I had hesitantly brought up going to a black salon after I got home from being with Reggie, she had read some Yelp reviews and gotten me an appointment for the next day, just like that. But I could tell she was nervous.

My stomach began to churn and my palms were hot. I grabbed my weathered copy of *American Gods* and got out of the car. Mom's hairdresser, a middle-aged white woman, was the only other person besides Mom who had done my hair. Usually, she somewhat fearfully trimmed up the ends.

Walking to the door of the new salon, my skin felt paper-thin, almost translucent. A sweetness overwhelmed my nose as we entered the waiting room, a pungent, chemical odor. Peeking over the divider, I saw three black women seated in high salon chairs, their heads encapsulated with Saran Wrap. One had huge thighs that burst from her shorts like bread rising in an oven; earrings the size of my fists hung from another's ears. The last one, who was more my color than the other two, was absently flipping through the pages of *Jet* magazine, sighing every now and then. Her eyes met mine suddenly, and it seemed like they were asking, "Who the fuck are you?" so I darted my head back into the waiting room, resolving firmly not to look at any one of them again. My fingers clasped *American Gods* even tighter. If things got really uncomfortable here, I could always retreat to my book.

"Alexandra Kirtridge," Mom was telling the woman at the counter.

She moved her light green fingernails down the pages of the datebook. "Ah, yes. Alexandra. I see you right here." She stuck out her hand. "You're my two o'clock. My name's Naomi, and I'll be doing your hair today."

"Nice to meet you," I heard myself say. I began to feel like I was in the middle of a game, up to bat, and the pitcher was about to throw me something I knew I had no chance of hitting. My fingertips tingled the same way they did then.

"So, I'll pick you up in about hour, then?" Mom said to me.

She turned to Naomi. "Will that be enough time?"

"Well," said Naomi, looking me over. "That depends on what she wants."

Mom had already grabbed her purse and turned on her heel, poised to leave. "Oh," she said, surprised. "Well, what do you want, Alex?"

They were both staring at me, waiting for me to say what it was I wanted. I could see that they needed to know right then, that it was urgent, that I should say something. *Tell them what you want.*

"I want it less frizzy."

Mom's eyelids fluttered slightly, and she stepped back—probably trying to get me in focus. Then she recovered and swept an imaginary hair out of her face. "Okay," she told Naomi. "Less frizzy."

But Naomi was not fooled. Her eyebrows knit together. She knew that I didn't know what I wanted. "You want it straightened? Is that what you mean? Do you want me to relax the curl a bit? Or maybe straighten it, and give you a set of rollers to take with you? I got some really fly extensions in this week that customers have been raving about. We could even put in a weave if you really want to try a new look. Just 'cause we live in the Midwest doesn't mean we can't be as fly as the coasts." She grinned at me, like we were both in on a joke.

Straightened, curled, re-curled, relaxed, weave. It was like a whole new language. I looked up at Mom, but her face only reflected my own questioning and uncertainty. I could see I would just have to pick an option and hope that it worked out; that was the best I could hope for.

"Relax the curl," I said, almost in a whisper. I liked the way the word sounded: *relaxed.* My curls were tightly wound like small springs, and in my mind I could almost see them becoming new, unfamiliar, cascading down my back in dark waves. Mornings I would rise from bed and shake them out, shaking not just my head but my shoulders also, like those women in Pantene commercials. I would trade my pick for a brush, one with a shiny gold handle, and when I sat at my bureau, I would run the brush all the way through, scalp to back. The brush wouldn't catch on any nasty curls, any split ends, like my pick did now. As Naomi walked me to the salon chair, Mom stood there in the waiting area, watching us. I could almost hear her say, as she always did, "You never know how something will be if you don't try it."

I sat down in the high swivel seat.

"Okay, let's get you going," Naomi said. She threw a plastic sheet around my body, and snapped it at the neck. Mom waved at me from the waiting room, moving toward the door to go. Naomi removed my barrette, and hair sprayed out behind me like a lion's mane.

"Girl, you got a lot of hair," Naomi said, with a laugh. She turned the pick over and began to divide my hair into sections using its sharp, pointed end.

My fingers clutched the armrests.

Naomi clipped the portion of my hair she had finished with a bright pink hair clip and started on another one.

"Does she know what to do with it?" she asked.

I closed my eyes. "Who?"

"Your mom," said Naomi. "She's your mom, right? The woman who dropped you off?"

Does she know what to do with it? "Yeah," I said. "I . . . I guess so." I willed my eyes open; I knew I needed to see what she was doing.

Naomi laughed. "You guess she's your mom, or you guess she knows how to do your hair?"

"She knew how to do it when I was little," I said. "But now I do it."

Naomi grabbed another hair clip and fastened it onto the section she had just finished dividing. Then she started on a new section, whipping my neck toward her. "And how do you do it?" she asked.

It wasn't at all like talking to Reggie; when he asked a question, it was like we were talking, not like I was an interesting and rare animal specimen.

"I dampen it with water every morning, then put on some hair gel," I said. "Then I usually pull it back."

"Hmm," she said. "Gel isn't good for hair like yours. Dries it out. Use some kind of leave-in conditioner."

Leave-in conditioner. Where would I find it? I would look for it in the black hair care section of Walgreens. Boxes and boxes of products with photos of women with the very same cotton-candy-style hair as Naomi.

She was leaning me back, I think in an effort to get a better angle on my scalp. "You never had a relaxer before, have you?"

"Nope."

"That's too bad," she said, clipping the last section. "Could've saved yourself a whole lot of trouble combing out this mess."

She need a black mother to tame that mess.

Naomi opened a violet package that had a smiling black girl with long, super straight hair across the front. I hiccupped.

"You okay?" Naomi asked. She was opening a container of something that looked an awful lot like shortening.

I hiccupped again. *I'm going to look beautiful.* "Yeah."

She stirred the white, plastic-like substance with a small wooden spoon, unclipped one section, and then began to smear it across my roots. "You don't have any scabs or open sores or anything on your scalp, do you?" she asked.

I frowned. "No."

"Okay, good," she said.

In the mirror, I saw that her finely manicured hands were covered in translucent plastic gloves, and I wondered if that was because what she was putting on my head was toxic. She must have sensed my uneasiness because she said, "It's nothing to worry about—all the chemicals are safe. You just want to try to avoid getting them into anywhere they shouldn't be." A fleeting image of Reggie's grandmom and her sparse hair came to me then, and I wondered if that was what your hair looked like after a lifetime of putting these "safe chemicals" on it.

The cream felt hot on my scalp, and it smelled like toilet bowl cleaner.

Naomi mashed the substance into a clump of hair and flattened it against my head with her gloves. "How does your head feel? Does it feel too hot?"

I shook my head. This was like a suicide sprint. I just had to get through it.

"Once you do it this one time, it's so much easier the next time, because you don't have to start all the way down at the roots," she said, moving on to another section of my hair and smoothing it straight as she went.

My scalp began to burn, but I knew I couldn't say anything. Maybe I had some scabs or bruises or something that I didn't know about. I looked sideways; she was getting to the bottom of the container. It would soon be over.

"Okay, now just sit here for a few minutes," said Naomi. She pulled a clear plastic cap over my head.

"Okay," I said, and watched in the mirror as she walked over to the receptionist and began to talk about nails.

I reached over and opened my book, praising myself again for remembering to bring it. It was amazing how many people didn't see you at all if you were lost in a book, or pretended to be. After a few minutes, however, I noticed that I had read the same paragraph three times. Both of the women who had had Saran Wrap on their heads when I walked in were now getting their hair washed of the chemical cream that had apparently done its work. Their hairdressers were rinsing their scalps with the highest pressure water I had ever seen. It was so loud that they were almost shouting through the salon.

"What, so she think she better than her sister?"

"Well, you know she got that good hair and high yellow complexion. All the mens be after her."

"Uh huh. But don't they got the same father?"

"Girl, you know she got that white daddy. She think she a child of Obama or something."

Laughter.

"Calling herself 'mixed' and all. Like there's some difference between the way white folks'll do a high yaller gal and a dark-skinned one."

"Girl, you right. She 'bout to find that out."

"Uh huh."

"Black is black is black is black. Has always *been* black, and always *will be*. I don't care what no one says."

"Everybody just got to think they better than someone else—'specially if they light. That's why we still can't get nowhere as a race."

"Now that's some real talk."

My ears were burning, and I concentrated intensely on the paragraph in front of me, wishing I could actually fall into the book. But it was futile; the language on the page could as well have been Russian for all I was understanding. Was it true? Did most mixed people think they were better than most black people simply because they were lighter and whiter? And what was the difference, the *important* difference anyway, between mixed people and black people? These women were saying that there really was none, that that was just something mixed people used to feel superior to black people, but I couldn't quite believe it.

I was sure that my hair was completely fried by the time Naomi came back for me, took me to a chair by a sink, and took off the clear plastic cap.

"Yeah, this is going to look so pretty," she said as she squirted shampoo into her gloved palm. Then she sat me back, pushed me up against the lip of the sink, and began to wash the cream out of my hair.

Her hands on my scalp felt so strange; I couldn't believe how easily they moved their way through my hair—catching on nothing. Reggie would no longer pull my curls and then let them bounce back.

Naomi washed all the shampoo out of my hair, shampooed and rinsed it again, and then squirted on something she called a deep conditioner.

"See," she said, sitting me up and turning me toward the mirror. "Beautiful."

I slowly looked up at the face in the mirror. It was a narrow face, much narrower than I had ever realized, with full lips and big, sad eyes. My hair was longer than I ever imagined it could be—running past my shoulders all the way down past my upper back. The crazy curls that defied both gravity and water were gone now, and in their place were long, stringy strands that left me feeling exposed and naked.

"It might take a minute to get used to because it's so different, but wait till you see it blow-dried," said Naomi. She squirted an oily substance in her hand, rubbed it on my hair, and then blew it dry. Then she went around me and snipped the ends off. Scissors. Creams. Oils. Blow drying. More scissors. Each new step in her process was another mystery to me, and before she'd finished them all, an hour had gone by.

"You just put this cream I'm going to give you on it every morning, and then blow it dry just like this, and then you're set, voilà!" she said, and then she made liked she was Vanna White and I was one of the letters she was turning over.

I stood up and peered at myself carefully. My hair was parted perfectly, right down the middle. The cut was layered in the front, with chic, jagged edges that framed my face. Naomi beamed at me in the mirror, obviously pleased with her work. Then I started to cry.

"What . . ." said Naomi, and she leaned closer to me. "Are you okay?"

All I could think was that I looked like an Indian—the kind you might see in a John Wayne movie. My hair, it suddenly occurred to

121

me, wasn't this straight because it wasn't supposed to *be* this straight. My face was too angular, my features too defined. It was all wrong. And now I would have to wait at least a year to get my hair back.

Naomi tried to hug me. "Honey, whatever it is, we can fix it."

I need to stop crying. But the more I tried to stop, the more the tears fell.

"Even if you want it back curly again, we can put curlers in it to make the curl even cuter than it was before—and less frizzy, too," Naomi was telling me. She looked at me hard. "You know, that's really what we should have done in the first place, anyway. You're right, maybe this is too drastic."

I covered my mouth with my hand, so that I wasn't exactly sobbing. I wished I could just run out of there, but home was a good twenty-minute drive away. This was the second time recently I had cried hard in public.

"Okay, yeah," said Naomi. "That's it, that's exactly what we'll do—we'll just give you a set of rods you can use every morning, it'll be easy. You won't even be able to tell the difference, except that the curl will be lighter, prettier." She clapped her hands. "Yeah, that's it." She bent down and began to rummage through the cabinets. "Just let me find that set . . ."

I need to stop crying. Now. Before Mom gets here. I wiped my eyes and face clean with the backs of my hands and took a deep breath. "No, no, it's okay," I told her. "Don't worry, I like it."

A woman at the hair dryer in a yellow jogging suit was staring right at me, her eyebrows knitted together in concern. Other women at the salon were beginning to notice all the commotion, too. It was definitely time to go.

Naomi turned away from the cabinet and looked at me incredulously. "You what?"

My heart, my heart. Heat rising from my chest, from deep down in there, the aorta and its ventricles, trying to contain this friction that just kept on bubbling up. My heart would burst, I was sure of it; I could see its red pieces splattered on the bright white walls. *I can breathe.* "I like it," I told her, sniffing. "I mean, it's different and everything," I faked a laugh, "but I'm getting used to it." I pushed out a smile.

Naomi crossed her arms and leaned back on a small table. "You're getting used to it," she said.

"Yeah," I said. The tick of the clock on the wall was like a new, tiny nail ramming my skull every second. I wanted to grab onto it; I thought that maybe its sound could keep my heart together.

Then Mom walked in the door.

CHAPTER
TWENTY-THREE

"Wow!" Mom clasped her hands over her mouth. "I just . . . cannot . . . believe it. You've done an amazing job, Naomi. She looks like a real, grown-up young woman now, doesn't she?"

Naomi looked at me questioningly, and I forced out a fake smile.

"Well, yes. I think it came out quite nice," she said.

"That's an understatement," Mom said, laughing. She came around the high barbershop seat and patted my hair down. "It's so soft, isn't it? I had no idea her hair was so soft. Or even that it could do this." She laughed again.

Women at the salon were beginning to notice the spectacle of us and give Mom the evil eye. Of course, she had no idea.

"I just can't believe it. We should have done this years ago."

I gingerly lifted her hand from my head and stepped down from the chair. "Mom, we better go." I pulled my cell from my pocket. "The time."

Mom laughed, a little too happily, I thought. She was almost as good at acting as I was. "Yes, you're right." She turned to Naomi. "How much do I owe you?"

. . .

When we got home, Dad and Jason could not stop talking about it. "It's fantastic," said Dad.

"It does look pretty damn good," said Jason, chomping on a handful of peanuts.

The rest of the day they came up behind me while I was getting a glass of water or watching TV and touched my hair very carefully. "It's so smooth," they said, smiling. "It doesn't even look like your hair."

I just smiled back at them. I couldn't tell them that it wasn't actually me they were looking at, that it was rather who I had wanted to be. I couldn't tell them that I wanted to take it all back, that I would have given anything for my crazy curls, because I was too embarrassed. I couldn't even admit this to Kit, who was, of course, less impressed by my new look than everyone else.

Her first response was a frown when she saw me. "What's that about?"

"By 'that' you mean this new haircut?" I asked.

"Yeah . . . or whatever it is," she said, peering at me sideways, like I was some kind of new zoo animal. "Is that really your hair? Or is it fake?" She shook her head. "Whatever. It just doesn't look like you. Sorry."

I laughed. "You're underestimating the value of looking like someone else. Sometimes it's better."

Kit stuck her tongue out at me. "And sometimes it's not," she said, and left the room.

By evening I had to get out of the house. Just moving, walking, could sometimes quiet my mind. I knew we needed milk, so I grabbed some change and quickly walked out the door before Mom had a chance to say anything.

Anil's Market was just six blocks away, but by the time I walked in, I felt like myself again. Walking by the oak trees and seeing their leaves blowing around in the wind but not falling down calmed me somehow. *Hair grows back.* Every time I pulled at my too-slick ponytail, I felt a little sick. So I put my hands in my pockets and tried to think of something else. Before long, I was remembering Reggie's touch and smiling to myself. Until I walked into the shop and spotted a group of black kids congregating at the counter. They weren't from West High, but they might as well have been. They lived in the neighborhood and watched me as I watched them: silently, and in judgment. I went straight to the back, where the cold stuff was housed in refrigerators, but it was already too late because they had seen me. I pulled at the ends of my ponytail. At least they couldn't come at me about my hair.

I opened the refrigerator and pulled out a gallon of two-percent milk. They were silent, taking me in as I walked up to the counter. I hadn't counted on seeing anyone of importance while running the errand, so I was wearing a five-year-old pair of faded jean shorts and a ratty T-shirt. My Tevas completed the look. I smiled at them and at their friend who was working the cash register. There were four of them: two girls who looked about my age, a guy who looked older, and another guy behind the counter. One of the girls rolled her eyes at one of the guys as I approached.

"Four fifty-six," said the guy behind the counter. He grabbed the milk and put it in a plastic bag. I dug in my pocket for the five I had grabbed.

"Nice shorts," the girl's voice came from behind me. The guy beside her laughed. My face burned.

"What are they, Jordache?" she continued, and the guys almost fell out. They were holding their sides, covering their mouths with their hands.

I put the five on the counter and waited for my change.

"She don't never speak," said the boy. "Maybe she mute or something." The girl giggled.

The kid behind the counter got himself together and cleared his throat. "Okay, enough already. She a paying customer. Let her alone."

The girl snickered. "Oh, Jamal's working for the Man now, he can't be playing with the likes of niggas."

I winced. Jamal handed me my change, and I picked up the bag and walked toward the exit.

"Your hair do look nice though," the girl called out as I pushed the door open. "You actually decent now."

I kicked sharp stones on the sidewalk all the way home, trying to cut my big toes, thinking about how Reggie could have been one of those kids. If he hadn't already known me from playing baseball, he probably would make fun of me just like all the others. He was nice to me, sure, but maybe just because he wanted something from me. *And he doesn't need anything from you anymore.* Had I really done it? Had I touched him, let him touch me everywhere? I punched my fist into my hip bone. *You are not the same; you will never ever be the same. He's probably out right now, telling everyone he knows about it.*

• • •

Reggie ran his cool, light fingers from my scalp to the base of my neck. "I can't believe you did it," he said.

I sighed. We were in his living room the next day, the television tuned to *Jeopardy*, but neither of us was really watching. "It was your idea." His touch made my skin prickle, deliciously.

He took his hand from my hair. "How can you say that?" His dark brown eyes looked genuinely hurt. "All I told you was about my mom and my sisters, and what they do. It wasn't meant as a *suggestion.* You were just going on and on about how you hated your hair, so I thought I'd offer you another option . . ."

I slouched down into the couch. "You don't like it, do you?"

Reggie reached for the bowl of chips on the coffee table in front of us. "I never said that." His biceps rippled nicely under his T-shirt.

127

I worried that he would catch me staring, so I looked away. "You didn't have to." *Yeah, this is going to look so pretty.* I laughed at the absurdity of it all. "There's really nothing to apologize for, anyway. I don't like it either."

He shoved a few corn chips into his mouth. "Really?"

I laughed again. "Yeah, really." My right hand moved toward his right arm, almost with a will of its own. *Stop. Now. You like him, but you are not what he really wants. Quit lying to yourself.* I ran my finger across his bicep, transfixed.

"Girl, what you doing?" he asked, crunching the chips.

I shrugged, repositioning myself on the couch so that I was facing him, straddling him with my knees. I kissed the top of his earlobe, then the middle, then the bottom.

He pulled me toward him, and pushed his hands up my shirt under my bra.

I shivered.

He pushed his hand down back the way it had come, so that it was fondling my ass. "Grandmom's taking a nap in the other room," he whispered in my ear. "Let's go to my room."

I nodded and moved myself off him, and off we went.

CHAPTER
TWENTY-FOUR

At the bottom of the house, trapped in a filing cabinet, my father's words spoke to me from decaying paper. That night, time stretched out and covered me, so that I thought I no longer had a body, so that there wasn't any such thing as my birth or my death, sex, conception, so that my parents had not even given me up, so that everything had happened, had always happened all at once, and I didn't have to choose or act. All of it, even my legs that couldn't keep up anymore, and my right arm that was no longer strong, would pass into oblivion anyway. Yet still, in the hot darkness of June, lying on top of my covers, sweating, he would not be silenced: *There was a lot of things that could have been better between your mother and I. I would have liked the chance to know you. This will be my last letter to you in awhile. I think I sent enough. Hopefully some day, when you're ready, we can see each other.*

"Shut up!" I said into the darkness. I pressed my hands over my ears and then sat up. The green light of my electric clock flashed in my eyes: 2:10 a.m. I moved to the edge of the bed, kicking at its side gently with my heels, like I used to do when I was a kid.

"He's not going away," I said, turning over my hand so that my palm faced me. Was it his? "He never left."

The next morning, I Googled his name and Detroit. It wasn't very difficult; the third name I clicked on and there it was:

Keith Mitchell, 2887 51st St., Detroit, MI, 313-995-4322.

The address looked the same as the one scrawled in the corner of those twenty letters I never received. I stared at the digits long and hard, not really believing that it had been so easy to find them. *I didn't even have to open a book on searching.* I didn't know much, but I knew that I was lucky.

It was afternoon before I felt ready. I picked up my phone. *Father, father, why did you do it?* The way I felt about him was the same way I felt about Reggie, I realized: I just wanted him. He was also the only key I had to my mother. I looked at my bedroom door, making sure that it was locked. *313-995-4322.* If I typed the numbers fast, I didn't even have to think about it. The phone rang; my grip on my phone tightened. *313-995-4322.* The phone rang again. Maybe no one was there.

"Hello?"

My lungs could have been collapsing. I had the feeling that I was falling on a roller coaster, weightless and headed straight for the ground.

"Hello?" the voice said. It was a young voice, filled with irritation. The wrong number? The wrong Keith? A landline?

"Is Keith Mitchell there?" I asked. My hand was getting sweaty, so I tried holding the phone with just my fingertips.

"Yeah, just a sec," said the voice, just like I was the pizza guy checking on a delivery or something. I heard the phone fumbled, then feet stomping, and then, "Dad! Phone!" *Dad?* It was probably only a few seconds, but it felt like five minutes before a heavier, more balanced set of feet shuffled to the phone. "Hello?" His voice was lower than I would have thought and also a little bit scratchy.

"Hi," I said. I kicked at my bedposts.

"Who's this?" he asked.

Your daughter. How are you? I stifled a laugh; the whole thing was ridiculous. Maybe I should just hang up.

"Look, I got things to do. So if you're a telemarketer, go bother someone else—"

"This is Alexandra Kirtridge," I blurted.

"You're . . . Who are you?" His voice changed; it was a little more hesitant.

"I'm Alexandra Kirtridge," I said. "You sent me letters." I was pacing across the carpet like it was my spot in center field.

"Alexandra?" His voice kept on getting quieter.

"Yeah," I said.

I heard some shuffling in the background and then a few doors shutting. I had the feeling he was moving into another room. "I wasn't expecting to hear from you," he said.

My stomach churned. This was a bad idea; I knew it. "I'm sorry, I—"

"No," he interrupted me. "It's not that. I want to talk to you. I . . . I been wanting to talk to you for sixteen years."

I exhaled slowly. *My father is still alive.* I think that was the first moment I had consciously contemplated that he could have been dead.

"Just after I got no answer to the letters, I didn't think I'd hear from you."

I bit my lip, trying to think of something to say. What he wanted was an explanation, and I didn't have one.

"I mean, I know I shouldn't have sent them in the first place, that that put you in a strange spot," he said.

"I just got the letters," I said. "Just now."

There was an audible pause. "Oh."

Someone laughed downstairs.

"So, you live in Detroit."

"Yup, the Motor City. Or at least, used to be," he said and then laughed. Nervous. Also slightly familiar. "You ever been?"

"No."

"You should come sometime. It's a great town—lots of good jazz, lots of good food and good people. And our baseball team ain't too bad, either."

I laughed, grabbing the Tigers like a lifeline. "Yeah, the Tigers, they always seem to be so close to winning it all."

Another awkward pause.

"So, you live in Madison," he said.

"Yes."

"Always seemed like a good place," he said.

"Yeah, it has its strong points," I said. I thought about mentioning the beautiful parks, the strong schools, all the items that everyone had to mention while bragging about Madtown to others, but everything sounded stupid in my ears. That was why the silence started off small but then grew bigger and bigger until I was afraid to say anything at all because it would not take up enough space to beat back the strangeness.

"Alexandra, you know," he was saying, before I realized it. "You're always welcome to come out here. To visit, I mean."

I winced. *To visit.* I would be a visitor.

"My mother. What is she like?" As usual, the question was out of me before I even had time to consider its effect.

He coughed. "Your mother . . . She was beautiful. And sad."

Was. I put my hand over my mouth, even though no sound was coming out.

"She shouldn't have died when she did," he said, and there was a touch of something—maybe anger—in his voice. "I told her a million times not to mess with that stuff, but she never listened. I tried to get her into rehab, but once she made up her mind, that was it."

Who was she? I closed my eyes and images of Charlize Theron and Angelina Jolie appeared, and then disappeared just as quickly. What remained was nothing. *There was enough pain having me. After that you went toward pain with your head thrown back and your mouth*

132

full of laughter. Your addiction was to forgetting me. The things you did to forget.

"Okay," I said. "Okay." I was trying to gather enough momentum to get up, grab a pen and paper, and write some of this down. Who knew when and if I would ever have the chance to get this kind of information again? But my legs seemed to be locked underneath me; I could not figure out how to move them.

I hadn't even known that I missed her.

"I know this must be a lot for you," he was saying.

I breathed in, and when my lungs reached capacity, I wanted to hold the air there forever; I never wanted to exhale again. "I have to go now," I told him. "I have to rest." I sat down on my bed, exhausted suddenly.

"Yeah," he said. "You should rest."

I lay back. "It was nice talking to you." That was the same phrase I used to get off the phone with my grandmother.

"You too," he said. Then he asked for my phone number, and I gave it to him.

I was just about to hang up when he said, "You should really come visit sometime. I would really like to meet you. And also have my family meet you. My wife and my daughter . . . I didn't even mention them, did I? Anyway, I know we'd all like to meet you. Please think about it, Alexandra."

"Alex," I said.

"What?" he asked.

"You should call me Alex."

He coughed. "Oh. Think about it, Alex."

"I will."

"Okay, then. Good-bye."

"Good-bye," I said, and gently placed the phone on the bed beside me. Then I got up, turned out the light in my room, and crawled under my covers. As evening fell, I tried to cry for my mother, but I couldn't. I was crying for myself, and for everything I had missed.

133

A girl in the library was watching me and had been for some time. She wasn't a girl, actually, but a young woman, with light skin and closely cropped hair that was wound even tighter than mine had been. She worked at the reference desk, and the button pinned to her shirt read "Kara."

"Unfortunately, most of these books are written for adults," a middle-aged, slightly frumpy-looking librarian was telling me. I had asked her to help me find books on adoption and reunion. The young woman, Kara, was diligently stacking returned books beside her, trying to look like she wasn't listening. "There doesn't seem to be much at all in the way of choosing for young adults," said the older librarian.

"Nothing?" I leaned into her screen.

She turned the screen toward me, so I could see. She frowned. "Not really. It looks like there is one book on general adoption issues for teens, but that's checked out."

I sighed. "Well, if you could just print out the list of adult books you have, that would be fine. I'm sure they apply in some way." *Anything is better than nothing. And if I am going to go to Detroit, I am not going out there empty-handed.*

The woman gave me a half-smile and apologized. "I think the problem may be that so few people search before they're of legal age, so there may not be a market for books like this. You're something of an outlier, I'm afraid."

I winced. "Tell me about it," I said under my breath.

The librarian handed me the printout, and I could see Kara struggling with herself over whether or not she should take this last chance and actually say something to me. Apparently, the louder side won, because she awkwardly leaned over the older woman and said, "I know of some other resources."

The librarian raised her eyebrows. "Oh?"

Kara ignored this, and instead, addressed me again. "I'm sorry to butt in like this, but I'm an adoptee myself, and I've gone through search and reunion. I can help you with a few things . . . I mean, if you want."

An adoptee? The words "adoption," "adopt," and "adopted" were familiar to me, and I had heard lots of people use them, but I had never heard anyone actually call *themselves* an "adoptee." It was strange to me, the idea of turning what others had done to you into a noun to describe yourself. "Yeah. Sure," I stammered. I felt my vision shifting out of focus again.

Kara lifted the gate between us and stepped beside me. The older woman looked at us with interest, decided her attention was better spent elsewhere, and turned back to her screen.

"Kara Murphy," she said, offering me her hand. I nodded, wanting more than anything to bolt and get out of there as quickly as possible. But if talking to her meant that I could get some information that might help the slow spread of panic in my chest every time I thought about Keith, then I could move my mouth, or listen and look interested forever.

"And you are . . ."

"Alexandra Kirtridge," I said. "I'm in high school." I don't know why I added that. Probably because it was a random and relatively safe piece of information that meant nothing.

If Kara thought I was strange for saying it, she didn't let on. She just nodded, took my arm, and gestured toward the other side of the room. We began walking.

"You said . . ." I cleared my throat. "You said you are an adoptee yourself." *An adoptee. I am an adoptee.*

She nodded, leading us through a set of double doors, into the stairwell. "Yes. I'm a transracial adoptee."

"A trans . . . ?"

Kara laughed. "Transracial adoptee," she said, slower this time. "A person of color adopted into a white family." We had reached the top of the stairs and walked into the main nonfiction area.

"Oh," I said. "Never heard that phrase before."

"Never met any other transracial adoptees then, huh?" She asked, guiding me down aisle 818.75 NS.

She didn't say it in a mocking tone or anything—it was just matter-of-fact. Still, I felt exposed and somehow inadequate for some reason, so I lied. "Oh, yeah. I do know quite a few. We just don't call ourselves that."

Kara raised an eyebrow but didn't say anything. I'm sure she knew I was lying.

We had reached the end of the aisle. Kara led me to a small computer lab and sat me down in front of a computer. She turned on the monitor.

"I love Fran, but she, like most older white folks, doesn't really know much about TRA culture," said Kara. The screen lit up and I pulled my chair in. "Sorry, Fran's the head librarian you were talking to."

I nodded.

"There's actually a lot of decent stuff online now. Ten years ago, no. But now you can find tons of blogs, some discussion boards, even adoptee-led magazines. Even the mainstream media thinks we're the hottest new thing. Even though we've always been here." She laughed and began to type something into the search engine.

There is a "we." There is an "us." It was like I had never even entertained the possibility. That I wasn't completely alone.

"Okay, so here's a list I like," Kara said, sitting back in her chair. She pointed to a long list on the screen, with links to pages called *Harlow's Monkey, Land of a Gazillion Adoptees,* and *A Birth Project.* "These are all blogs for and by adoptees."

I blinked at the screen. "Really?"

"Yep," she said. "Some of them are international adoptees, some of them domestic. Some are young like you, some are older, some are more personal, others more scholarly."

My head was spinning. I was still trying to make sense of the fact that there were more of us.

"Some people are talking about search and reunion, others

about redefining their relationship with their adoptive family, and others are discussing dating as an adoptee. So I think you should be able to find some insight and support for any issue around the adoption experience here," she said.

It was a little like talking to a teacher but infinitely more useful. I found some of the terms she was using, and their context, completely unfamiliar, but it was fascinating to realize that there was a whole field of study on this topic. "Thank you," I said slowly. "This is really helpful."

She nodded, leaning back in her chair. Everything about her— her wide shoulders, long fingers and finely manicured fingernails—oozed confidence. Perhaps she was twenty-five, almost thirty? Maybe this was how I would look at that age. *That would not be bad at all.*

Kara stood up. "I have to go back to work now, but here's my e-mail address and cell number." She ripped off a small piece of scratch paper and scribbled down the info. "You can always write, call, or text me if you have another question." She smirked. "We're already too alone as it is." There was some heat behind these words, and I wanted to ask her what she meant exactly. I wanted to hear her story. Did she make contact with her birth parents? What were her adoptive parents like? Did she fit in anywhere? But we had only just met, and these were not conversations that strangers had.

"I'll do that," I said, grabbing the paper possessively. "Definitely."

Kara turned on her heel and walked away, back toward the stairwell. She walked like she owned the place, and maybe she did. I was sure that this wasn't the only thing she knew more about than the head librarian.

I faced the computer and sighed. Where to begin? I finally just clicked a link, any link, and began reading.

"I have asked the agency a million times for my birth records, which they still insist were burned down in a fire shortly after I was born. There is no record of such an event, however, so I know they are lying," one woman wrote on her blog. "It's like they think they rescued me from some treacherous Third World childhood in Bangladesh," another wrote, "and that they believe that I should be endlessly thanking them for this 'rescue,' this access to First World education, health care, housing, and amenities. But what about everything else I missed, and am still missing because they took me from my home? What about my language? My food? My culture? What about my birth family?"

And one blog finally unraveled for me the mystery of my "special needs" status at the time of my adoption:

The narrative of colorblindness which most white adoptive parents strictly adhere to is flawed in many respects, which I have explored in detail in previous posts. But one of its most serious contradictions lies in the reality of the market for children, whose monetary 'value,' both in domestic and international markets, is largely determined by their race. More specifically and insidiously, the lighter you are, the more you will cost, because there will be more demand for you. Such are the consequences of doing the 'business' of child welfare in the capitalist context, which has always been (if not overtly, then covertly) racist. Black children, especially those marked with some disability, are consistently the cheapest, followed by mixed children, and Native and Latino children, then Asian children. At the top of the Available for Adoption food chain lies The Healthy White Infant—that ever-elusive treasure that so many white adoptive parents would give almost anything to attain. This is why so many children of color were, and in some cases still are, labeled as "special needs," by state agencies, thus putting them in a category with lowered (incentivized) adoption fees for prospective parents. It is a way to combat these racist market forces, and make black, mixed, Latino, and Native children more 'attractive' to potential 'buyers,' i.e., adoptive parents.

I gasped. So, simply being black or mixed, or just not white made you "special needs" in the eyes of these agencies and their clients? What did this mean about me and my parents? Did they then somehow see me in these terms as well? Was I somehow "less valuable" to them than Jason or Kit because I wasn't white, because they had gotten such a "deal" on me? It was disgusting to think of family like this, but on the other hand, it was hard not to, given this information.

Browsing blog after blog, I had the oddest feeling. Like all this time, I thought I was a freak, an aberration of nature, born with a skin that wasn't my own. But now, I began to wonder if I was actually just an archetype. Maybe this loneliness and shame, this fear of being discovered as not truly black, were just part of what it meant to be a "transracial adoptee." And if so, there was maybe another way out of it, another side to the experience.

After three and a half hours in front of the monitor, my eyes were bleary and my stomach was rumbling. I'd missed a whole weight-training session. All of the blogs, the sites, the voices, had given me some perspective on meeting Keith but also on my family. I saved all of the sites on my phone before I left.

As I drove back home, I reflected on the fact that I might not be as much of a freak as I always thought I was. Maybe I just belonged to an outlaw tribe. One that you wouldn't even know was there unless you knew how to go looking for it. And maybe, those of us in the tribe weren't responsible at all for what had happened to us, all the things that had made us who we were. Maybe we actually had nothing to apologize for. To anyone.

CHAPTER
TWENTY-FIVE

Kit and I sometimes went to the kiddie playground just a few blocks away. We liked to sit on the swings that almost dropped to the ground under our weight and twist and turn the chains, spinning ourselves back and forth. The motion reminded us of some part of ourselves we tended to forget in our house and made us giddy at the same time.

"I knew it," Kit said, when I told her about Kara. "I knew you couldn't be the only one."

I nodded. "Of course I'm not the only transracial adoptee in Madison." I spun myself fast to the right, unwinding my chain and almost flinging myself off the swing. The words *transracial adoptee* still felt strange in my mouth, but I was getting more used to hearing them. "It's logical . . ." I frowned. "But also strange."

Kit rammed her swing into mine. "Strange like how?"

I moved back a little, so her swing missed mine. "Like there's all these people out there who are walking around feeling like just as much of an imposter as you do, and you never knew it."

She laughed. "You're not an imposter."

I looked away from her, at the violet beginning to pierce the night sky. "I am to most black people." I sighed. "You don't get it. You're white."

She stopped ramming my swing for a minute and looked hurt. "Yeah, I'm white, but . . . I don't fit in either. We're both different."

I started to kick at the dirt, pushing my toes in deep, and slowly turning myself in a clockwise motion. "We're both different but not in the same way. I can't explain it."

Kit frowned. "You're uncomfortable being uncomfortable."

I let go of my twisted-up chain and spun crazily, as fast as I could. "Yeeee!" I yelped as the wind smacked my cheeks.

"I'm comfortable being uncomfortable," she said. "Maybe that's the difference."

I felt anger bubbling up in my stomach. "You don't have black kids in your face every damn minute teasing you because you don't talk right or don't have the right hair. You don't stick out at all— you blend right in with everybody. And everybody thinks you're so fucking beautiful, too." I looked down at my scuffed up sneakers. "They always have."

"I don't care what they think!" Kit exclaimed. "That's on them."

I rolled my eyes. "See, that's what I mean. Kara and the others— I think that they would understand what I'm trying to tell you. I wouldn't have to explain it and then be misunderstood."

That stopped her. She looked sorry then. "I know it's not the same, being in your body and being in mine. I know that."

I got off the swing, dusting off my shorts. It was time to go. "It's good that you know it," I said. "Because no one else in our family does."

Kit jumped off the swing and ran over to me. She hooked her arm in mine, and we slowly made our way back toward home. I got the feeling she was thinking hard. "Well, you're right. No one in our family knows that there's at least two realities in the world: black and white. But maybe your *other* family knows it. Maybe your father knows it."

I kicked at a stone, not sure what to say about that at all. "Maybe."

CHAPTER
TWENTY-SIX

I used the birthday money my grandmother had given me to pay for gas. It was a seven-hour drive to Detroit. I told my parents I was spending the weekend in Milwaukee with a friend from school, her mom, and her mom's best friend. The three of us usually made the trip once every summer, so it wasn't that much of a reach. My parents didn't even question it, and I was surprised that it wasn't even hard to lie to them. Dad had only asked that I keep up my training over the weekend since the state tournament was just a week away. I didn't even bother asking him if he was going to play me.

During the drive, I mulled over what I would say to Keith when we met. For years, I had been imagining what it would be like to meet my black father, the side of me that had always been the hardest to dig out. My father would be blacker than I because no part of him was white and (more importantly) because he was raised by black people. Black skin and kinky hair were one thing, but a black mind was another. When a black person saw another black person on the street, they expected them to share certain ideas with them about white people, about speech, even about the way they walked. When a black person saw me on the street, they expected the same. But I didn't talk like many of them, and my hair was nothing like theirs. Worst of all, my family was white. The question was, did I have a black mind? And if I didn't, could my black father help me make it black?

Though I had been happy and relieved about the success of my travel plans (and also how good it felt to deceive my parents after they had been deceiving me all these years), it wasn't long before I began to worry about the potentially explosive situation I was walking into. On the phone the night before, Keith had assured me that his wife and daughters were really looking forward to meeting me. I knew he could tell me anything he wanted to about what his wife and daughters thought about me (or the idea of me at this point, anyway), but the reality could easily be different. They might resent me; they probably would. Who was I, anyway, but some remnant from my birth father's life that he had never properly disposed of? Someone who was still learning how to do her hair properly because no one could show me how to—or no one *chose* to, I corrected myself. Someone who didn't even know how she was black.

• • •

As I stood on the doorstep of their modest stucco ranch in Southeast Detroit at 5:31 p.m., this doubt finally overflowed in my mind and shook my fist, which I had raised to the door. The door was a fleshy pink color, and the paint was peeling. I pushed my knuckles against the wood and made myself hit it, hard. My stomach had begun to churn the moment I pulled up to their house, and I knew that I would have to be very careful and calm myself down fast, or a spasm of hiccups would be the Mitchells' first introduction to me. The door flew open.

"Hi." A woman in her mid-forties, with chin-length, straightened hair, and nails like talons greeted me. She wore a fuchsia silk shirt and pants set, pastel-colored eye shadow, and lipstick that shone brightly in the dying sunlight.

I smoothed my flowered skirt, could almost see the reflection of my plain and naked face in her eyes. "Hi," I said.

The woman wasn't smiling, but she wasn't frowning either. In fact, it was hard to determine exactly what was going through her mind. She held the door ajar, with just enough space for her small, slight frame. There wasn't possibly enough room for me to pass by her and enter the house.

I fiddled with my fingers and tried to imagine myself back home. "I'm Keith's daughter," I said, because I didn't know what else to say. "I mean his first daughter." I winced. "I mean, his daughter from a previous . . ."

"I know who you are," the woman said evenly. Then she opened the door and stepped to the side.

My stomach fell; I had been right. She didn't want me there. Maybe I should just turn around and go home. I hesitated on the doorstep, but almost against my will, my feet moved me forward.

A heavy brass mirror hung on the opposite wall, which was painted the same awful fleshy color as the door. There was one tiny window in the hallway, almost completely covered by royal blue velvet curtains. The overall effect was that of a fun house; it was creepy in a campy sort of way.

The woman stepped behind me and shut the door. Now that I was safely inside, I wanted to leave more than anything. I reached up to my hair, which I had collected in a tight bun at the back of my head. At least they couldn't have a quarrel with that.

Mrs. Mitchell eyed my small duffel bag, slung over an arm. "You can put that right over here, by the couch," she said, gesturing toward the corner. "You'll be sleeping on the pull-out couch tonight."

"Thanks," I told her and dropped the duffel in the corner.

"Ma, is she here? Is that her?" a voice called from down the hall. "She thin as Dad thought she would be?"

I felt my face color.

The woman was watching me. "Yes, she's here, Maya," she said. "Right here in the foyer."

I heard a giggle from behind a wall. Then a door opened, and a face peered at me. I tried to study the face to see if it looked anything like mine, but she was too far away. "Sorry," she said. "Not trying to say anything about thin folks. Wish I was one of them." She stepped out of the room so I could see all of her. She was shorter than me, maybe 5'4", and had wide hips, a round face, and the beginnings of breasts. Her hair was straightened, like her mother's, and her skin was the color of oak. She had to be thirteen or fourteen.

"It's good to be thin," said Mrs. Mitchell. She was 5'2" and couldn't have weighed more than a hundred pounds. "All my kin is thin."

Maya laughed. "Not all," she said.

Mrs. Mitchell rolled her eyes.

"Give it a rest already, Ma," Maya said. She turned toward me and smiled, and it was a wide, generous smile. Something about her reminded me of Kit. "It's Alex, right?" She held her hand out toward me.

I felt the muscles in my neck relax a bit. "Yeah," I said. He must have told her the name I preferred. I shook her hand.

I hiccupped and then covered my hand with my mouth, almost instinctively.

Maya's hazel eyes sparkled mischievously. "Hiccups, huh?" she asked.

Mrs. Mitchell folded her arms across her chest and tried to smile. "Why don't we sit down at the table? Everything's ready." She gestured for me to follow her, so I did. We walked through a dimly lit hallway that was plastered in photos. Everyone was smiling widely in the photos; every woman's hair was straightened, and

146

every man's hair shaved close to his head. In the corner at the end of the hallway, I saw a glass case containing what looked like at least fifty miniature crystal unicorns. Some were clear, others pink- and blue-tinted. Maya noticed me watching and laughed. "That's our unicorn shrine," she said. "Mine and Ma's. We been collecting them since I was three. Aren't they something?"

I leaned down so that I could get a better look. Afternoon sun- light from a nearby kitchen window shone in and bounced off the sharp and rounded corners of the animals. The unicorns sparkled as they pranced, stared, and slept. Some were grinning and others looked strangely placid. I was conscious of Maya's eyes at my back as I examined them, but I couldn't feel what she was thinking.

"They're really something," I said, rising. *Really something strange.*

Mrs. Mitchell turned and gestured around the corner. Her face was as somber as it had been when she first opened the door. "This way," she said.

My legs suddenly felt like they were underwater, pulling so much weight with each step. Why had I come here? I hiccupped again.

"You know, Dad hiccups when he's nervous, too," said Maya.

I spun around to face her, my face hot with surprise. There was a tightening in my stomach, but not from embarrassment; from excitement. Maya's eyes glittered with laughter. This was some- thing like Grandpa's, Dad's, Jason's, and Kit's eyes, how they all were connected by the same, cloudy gray color. I had hated the hiccup response for years, and now I wanted to somehow cut it out of me and keep it in a box, to carry around and show everyone whenever I wanted to.

Maya nodded. "Grandma Mitchell too. That's funny, huh?"

"Yeah," I said. Before I could say more, a hand grabbed my elbow and pulled me around the corner, then spun me around. The room was lit with candles; a tiny bouquet of wildflowers sat in the center of the table. There were six places set with fine china and shining silver utensils.

"This is our dining room," said Mrs. Mitchell. "Please have a seat."

Heavy footsteps clumped down the hallway. "We're ready to eat!" A young girl who looked about eight flew into the room.

"Jordan, stop yelling!" Mrs. Mitchell yelled. "We have a guest."

Jordan, who had cornrows decorated with translucent multi-colored beads, screeched to a halt in front of me. She pushed her glasses up the bridge of her nose, looking me over. "You don't look like Grandpa," she said.

I hiccupped again, then put my hand in front of my mouth.

Her eyes, which were light hazel, widened. "You hiccup?" She clapped her hands. "Grandpa hiccups too!"

Mrs. Mitchell rolled her eyes. "Jordan," she said. "You didn't even introduce yourself." She gestured toward the girl. "Alex, this is Jordan, my granddaughter. She's staying with us this month while my daughter Kylie is on vacation."

I nodded; I had no idea Mrs. Mitchell had had another daughter before she met Keith. This made me feel a little less strange in their house—I wasn't the only distant relative.

Jordan leaned into me, and began to whisper. "Grandpa got a big, wide nose, like Maya, and he don't like a child to interrupt him, especially when he's eating, so make sure you just eat quietly, to yourself."

"Jordan!" Mrs. Mitchell exclaimed. "Enough! We are sitting down to dinner."

Jordan pulled back and fixed her eyes on her grandmother. It was as if she had just noticed her standing there. "Well, where's Grandpa?"

That was the question that I had been wanting to ask ever since arriving.

"That's not your concern," said Mrs. Mitchell. "You need to sit down at the table and get ready for dinner."

Jordan put her hands on her hips, and shifted her weight to one foot. "She came to see Grandpa, didn't she? How am I going to sit down, ready for dinner if Grandpa's not here?"

Mrs. Mitchell rolled her eyes, but I could see she was suppressing a small smile.

The front door slammed in the other room. "I'm back!" It was the voice of my father. "I got the bread."

"Please," Mrs. Mitchell told me, gesturing to the table again. "Sit down."

It was a command more than a request, so I nodded and walked toward the table as lightly as I could. Jordan broke from Maya's arms and ran to me. "I'm sitting by you," she said, pulling me to the far end of the table. "Let's sit . . . here." She pulled out the chair on the left end of the table and pointed to it.

There wasn't anything to do but sit down. So I did, and Jordan scrambled to situate herself right beside me.

"They didn't have wheat so I got French," said Keith, walking down the hallway. "I hope it's okay . . ." His voice trailed off when he turned the corner and saw me sitting at the table. "Alex! You're early!" He was smiling. *The sound of his voice is the sound of his words. Those words on the paper were also his arms and his legs and his head and his eyes staring at me now.* He was taller than I'd expected, at least five inches taller than me—6'1" or 6'2". He had muscular arms, although the beginning of a belly poked out from under a thin dress shirt. But his face was kind, and in that way, reminded me of Reggie's.

Mrs. Mitchell snickered. I was grateful that her attention was no longer focused on me. "She's not early," she told Keith. "You're late."

Keith looked at his feet, but I could still see his jaw sagging. "Traffic," he said slowly, and with considerably less enthusiasm. "Traffic was a bitch."

Jordan elbowed me and hissed, "He said 'bitch'!" Then she covered her face with her hand and started to giggle. I told myself not to look at her because I knew that I might start laughing, too.

Mrs. Mitchell looked like she was going to say something else, probably scold him for swearing, when Maya said that everyone should sit down, that she and Ma had prepared a beautiful dinner. I could see that trying to keep track of everything and everybody would be difficult, if not impossible here. Things moved a lot faster than they did at my house.

Keith smiled at Maya, almost gratefully. "Good suggestion, pumpkin," he said. Then he told me he was sorry to be late.

After Maya, Mrs. Mitchell, and Keith all found seats around the table, Jordan was asked to say grace. She clasped her tiny hands together and bowed her head.

Jordan was right; Maya and Keith did have the same nose. It was flat and wide, almost touching the edge of their cheekbones. Her earlobes, however, were unattached at the bottom, like mine, but Keith's were not. And my ears lay flat against my head while Maya's and Keith's were bigger and stuck out a little. Maya was my half-sister, I realized.

"In the name of the father, son, holy spirit, amen," Jordan began. Her eyes were tightly closed, and her voice had taken on a deep, somber tone. I scrambled to clasp my hands and bowed my head. "Bless us oh Lord, and these thy gifts, which we are about to receive, from thy bounty, through Christ, our Lord. Amen."

"Amen," said everyone. Then they began to cross themselves. Trying to appear like I did this every day, I crossed myself also.

"Does your family pray before meals?" Mrs. Mitchell asked.

I felt like I had been caught shoplifting. I wanted to pretend I had answered already; I wanted to lie. "We don't usually," I said finally, "But I can."

I wasn't sure about how I felt about organized religion, though I always resented the inevitable proselytizing we received from Grandma Kirtridge whenever we went to visit her. Dad thought it was all "a bunch of bull to keep people separate, self-righteous, and cowardly," so we had never prayed or been to a church service in our lives.

Mrs. Mitchell and Keith exchanged glances. I had given an odd answer to her question, and I don't think they knew quite what to make of it.

"You don't pray in your house?" Maya asked. She seemed to genuinely want to know.

"Well, no, not exactly," I said.

She stared at me. "Do you go to church? What religion are you?"

My hand was dancing under the table. "Well, we don't really have one, though our grandmother is Christian."

Mrs. Mitchell smiled. "Your grandmother's Christian? What denomination?"

I tried to remember if my grandmother was Protestant or Catholic. She had probably told me a million times, but now, for some reason, it was eluding me. Keith and Mrs. Mitchell looked as interested in this line of questioning as Maya.

Under the table, Jordan grabbed my jumping hand and steadied it. I squeezed her back.

"She's Catholic," I said. "And we were baptized Catholic. Our parents just never had the time to take us to church. We're a busy family." I hiccupped again and put my hand over my mouth. "Sorry," I said.

Keith didn't acknowledge that he had heard either the hiccup or my apology. I couldn't remember if the story I had just told was true, if we had been baptized when we were babies. Something about it sounded vaguely familiar, but I couldn't pinpoint what.

"Well, we're Catholic," said Mrs. Mitchell, reaching for a bowl of tossed salad.

I nodded, mostly because I didn't know what else to do. For the first time, I noticed the polished oak cross on the opposite wall. There was also one in the foyer, I recalled, hanging above a mirror.

Maya passed me a steaming bowl of basmati rice. Keith picked up a platter of lemon chicken, and selected a fat piece. The room was quiet for a moment while everyone focused on passing and serving. Under the table, Jordan didn't let go of my hand.

Mrs. Mitchell was the one who broke the silence. "You know, our church is so important to us," she said. "I don't know how any

151

of us would have made it this far without it, or without our belief in the Lord Jesus Christ. We've had so many challenges."

I shivered. The way she said it, The Lord Jesus Christ, made him sound like an intimate lover, almost. I knew you weren't supposed to love a human being as much as Jesus if you believed in him, and so I wondered how Mrs. Mitchell meted out her love for Keith.

"What kind of challenges?" Jordan asked.

I snuck a look at her from the side but couldn't see a trace of sarcasm or malignancy. It seemed like a question that she actually wanted to hear the answer to.

Mrs. Mitchell's chin shot up, but she wouldn't acknowledge Jordan. She looked at me.

"Keith lost fourteen years of his life to alcoholism," she said. "In fact, he almost died from the disease." She watched me for my reaction, but I was trying to emit nothing.

"I'm also a recovering alcoholic. I've been sober for ten years now. Keith's been sober for nine."

Jordan's hand gripped mine tightly; it felt like my bones were crushing together.

I had heard once that there are certain people whose lives are governed by extremes, extreme indulgence on one end, and extreme asceticism on the other.

"AA, our church, its pastor, and of course praying got us up out of that life," Keith said. Mrs. Mitchell took his hand. I had been confounded about what tied them together, but now I could see it. "I surely would be dead by now, except for all those people, and a little help from the Almighty," he continued, smiling uncomfortably.

I wondered what he thought about the fact that this was the first thing I learned about him.

"So don't drink," he said suddenly, pointing his fork at me. "That's your lesson."

Mrs. Mitchell laughed, but I didn't think it was funny.

"No, seriously, hon, do you drink?" he asked.

I shook my head. I had never been attracted to drinking or drugs, mostly because the idea of putting something in my body that I couldn't control terrified me. But now I was thinking that there could be another reason why I never drank; maybe Keith had encoded specific messages in my nerve synapses that would fire whenever the opportunity to do so presented itself. There was such a thing as genetics, predetermined factors written in the body, so why not? Anything was possible.

Keith sawed his chicken in half. "That's good," he said. "Don't start."

I nodded, but it all felt ludicrous. My father, who wasn't really my father, instructing me to say no to drugs at our first meeting in all of my sixteen years.

It dawned on me that they were even less prepared for this moment than I was. They had no script for an adopted daughter reunion. They knew how to have a nice Saturday night dinner, though, and so that's what they had done.

"Would you like to come to church with us tomorrow morning?" Mrs. Mitchell asked me. "Nine o'clock mass is beautiful; we got some kind of choir." She turned to Keith for support, and he nodded but wouldn't look at me.

I shifted around in my chair and stared down at my food. What had happened to all of the questions I had been so determined to ask? How did I manage to get ensnared in nine o'clock mass?

"Alex probably has a million other things she's doing tomorrow," said Maya. She raised her eyebrows toward me. "Don't you?" I shot her a meaningful glance that I hoped she interpreted as "thank you."

"Yeah . . . yes," I said, grinding the gears of my mind. "I've got to finish several workouts in preparation for the state tournament, plus, uh, debate club Sunday night." The part about the workouts was true. Debate club? I had no idea where that came from, especially since it was summer vacation.

Maya eyed me suspiciously. "That's a lot."

I went too far. "Yes," I said. "It is."

Jordan loosened her grip on my hand under the table.

I addressed Keith. "What did you . . ." What was I saying? What was it I had promised myself I would say, again? I closed my eyes and took a deep breath. When I opened them, everyone at the table was watching me in bewilderment. Everyone except for Jordan—she was grinning like she was at some kind of show. This was it; this was the moment.

"Did you not think of me as black?" I blurted out. This might be my only chance. "I mean, since my mother was white and every-thing. Was that the reason why you gave me to a white family?"

Silence pervaded the room. My eyes were locked with Keith's, whose expression was one of shock and confusion. Maya's fork clanged onto her plate, and Jordan jumped at the noise. Mrs. Mitchell tilted her head back and said, "I don't know what you mean."

Jordan pulled her hand out of mine. "I thought you *were* black," she said.

Maya picked up her fork and pushed some rice onto it.

"You look black to me," Jordan continued.

"Jordan!" Mrs. Mitchell chastised. "That is not appropriate."

Jordan didn't even acknowledge that her grandmother had said anything.

I wouldn't look at Jordan or Mrs. Mitchell; my eyes were locked with Keith's, who was not responding at all.

Jordan leaned over and put her face near mine. "If I saw you on the street, I'd think you're black."

Maya grabbed Jordan's arm sharply and pulled her back down into the seat. "Stay in your seat at the table, I've told you before!"

Jordan rubbed her arm and whimpered. Her bottom lip was sticking out. "You hurt me," she said softly.

"I never got a chance to say what kind of family you'd be adopted into," Keith said suddenly, venom biting each word. Mrs. Mitchell and Maya were staring at him like he was a complete stranger. I guess at that particular moment, he was.

"She didn't give me hardly no choice in anything, Janie." He shook his head. "Told me she was pregnant and was going to have the baby, and I said we should get married. She said no, that we were neither of us fit to raise a child and that she was going to give it up and that was the last I heard about it." His face was taut and tired. "Until she mailed me a clipping from the paper years later, something about your dad and your family, and then I knew who you were. She didn't give me no decision about anything. Nothing." His bottom lip was quivering—not as much as Jordan's was, but quivering just the same.

Maya looked like someone had slapped her across the face. We were not half-sisters, I realized. There was no word for what we were to each other.

"Anyway, the most important thing is that a child be raised under the eyes of God," said Mrs. Mitchell. She looked absolutely unfazed. "No matter what color the family."

"But even if you're light, you're black," Jordan insisted. "Everyone knows black and white make brown." She frowned.

"Young lady, that's enough!" Mrs. Mitchell yelled.

Jordan's eyes filled with tears, and she started to bawl.

I looked down at my rice and salad and chicken. My stomach churned and I felt nauseous. "I'm sorry," I said. "I didn't mean . . ."

Maya handed Jordan a napkin to dry her eyes and she began dabbing at their edges. "It not fair," said Jordan.

"Life's not fair," Maya and Mrs. Mitchell said at the same time. I put down my fork. I hadn't planned on leaving until tomorrow morning, but I had booked a room at a hotel nearby, just in case this didn't work out. There was a way out, even if this visit wasn't what I'd hoped for. "You know, maybe I should go," I said. I nodded. "I mean, I didn't mean to upset everyone . . ." I heard my voice drift off and then I hiccupped.

Keith had been staring down at his plate, but after this last comment, he looked up at me in surprise. "You hiccup?" he asked. This time, he had obviously heard it.

I hiccupped again. "Yeah," I said. "Usually when I'm nervous."

"Or when you just feel bad, right?" he said, a slow smile pouring out the side of his mouth.

I nodded, carefully holding my stomach.

"Yeah, well, me too," he said. "And my mother, and my uncle Freddie, and his daughter Jasmine, and a whole truckload of Mitchells."

Jordan had stopped crying. She looked from me to Keith to me again.

"You ever try standing on your head to get rid of them?" he asked me.

"I've tried everything," I said. Then I thought about it. "Except that, I guess." I laughed, in spite of myself.

"Well, next time, try that," he said. "Works like a charm."

I still felt so strange, sitting there in my father's living room with his family, pretending that we knew each other. "I'll do that," I told him.

His eyes stared into mine, and I could see tears in their depths. *There is no language to explain what has happened to us. There is nothing that can replace what is gone.* I looked back down at my plate because I couldn't look at those eyes anymore. I got ready to tell them goodnight.

"Eat your chicken," Keith said, pointing to my half-eaten plate with his fork.

I looked into his eyes again and the tears had faded to the background. *Forget everything. Let me die in your mind like I did before and forget that this night ever happened.*

"Go on," he said. "Eat now, girl. You can't be coming all this way and not eat all this good food my wife and daughter prepared."

Maya nodded. "You can't be going back to Madison hungry," she said. "That would make us look like we got no home-training down here in Detroit. You can't let us go out like that."

I turned to Mrs. Mitchell, and she nodded. "Eat," she said simply.

I took a deep breath, picked up my fork and knife, and began sawing into my chicken. Every one of the Mitchells picked up their forks after me and continued eating as well.

• • •

In the middle of the night, I pulled the covers up to my nose and pushed myself as far onto the edge of the pull-out couch as possible. I wanted to be exposed. Like I was about to fall down onto the floor and bruise or break something. I didn't really want to get hurt. I think I just wanted Keith to see that I was as broken as he was. That I had no idea what I was doing, but that I was willing to take whatever pain and consequences might follow from whatever our relationship was. Or maybe I just wanted to see and feel my brokenness for myself—not just hold it in my mind.

I had thought that my reunion could bring so many possibilities: connection, finally a sense of belonging, or even confusion. But one thing I had not considered was that it would intensify this ache in me that everything in my life would never really fit together. As I rolled over in my makeshift bed at my birth father's, at 2:17 in the morning, I began to contemplate that things might never coalesce, and I wondered if there was a way that this could be okay.

• • •

The sky was clear blue over I-94, and I could see for miles on all sides. It was mid-afternoon, and I only had a few hours left on the road. I actually almost regretted it. It had been so long since I had been on a road trip, and I had forgotten how nice it was to just take off and go, even if you had a destination.

Your father wanted you, he always wanted you. Even though I was alone, I reflexively lowered my glance so that no one could see the tears gathering in my eyes. *Mom and Dad love me, but they don't know what to do with me. And I don't know what to do with them.* I stiffened and gripped the steering wheel tighter. And out of nowhere, the thought came: *Baseball is not the only thing in the world. The world is large. There are more uses than that for my body.* I passed a car on the left, and then signaled to come back over to the right lane.

The first thing I'd do, I decided, when I got home, was call Reggie and tell him everything. I wanted to see his face change from disbelief to worry to excitement as I told him about eating dinner with Keith, about how he hadn't had any say in my adoption, about how I thought I would visit them again, even though I knew I would probably never feel completely comfortable around them—especially because I wasn't a Christian. I wanted to apologize for not telling him everything before and explain that I was scared, that I had always been scared. I decided I would begin my journey back home by finally telling him the truth: I was starting to love him.

CHAPTER TWENTY-SEVEN

When I entered the house, Dad was bent over the table, poring over papers and playbooks scattered everywhere. I stood—watching him—really noticing him. It felt like I was watching a complete stranger. He didn't notice me standing there till the door shut behind me.

"Hey you," he said, turning toward me. His eyes brightened and he set down the pen. "How was it?"

For the first time, I really saw my father. His hair was graying on the sides and his hairline receded more each season. Purple bags hung under his eyes and the lines around them were growing deeper. I wondered how my father could have gotten so old without me even noticing.

"Milwaukee was fine," I lied, dropping my duffel onto the floor. "Good." I scanned his face for any sign that he knew I was lying, but I could find nothing. That was one thing I had always been thankful for: reading Dad was as natural and easy to me as breathing.

"We hit the Afro Fest and the Celtic Fest," I said, picking two of Milwaukee's festivals at random. I had no idea if they were actually held that weekend, but the city had so many festivals every season no one could keep track anyway.

"Food any good at either of them?" he asked.

I shrugged. "It was okay. We mostly ate at those high-end restaurants that Mrs. Adams likes." Mrs. Adams, my friend's mother, did have extravagant taste in food and was constantly arguing with my friend over whether she could have a corn dog or a portobello mushroom panini for lunch.

Dad stood up and walked toward me. I wasn't sure why. "Well, I have to admit that I'm glad to hear it. I'm going to need you as fresh and healthy as possible for Tuesday's game, and you'll need plenty of good food in your system for that." Tuesday: The quarterfinals, the first day of the state tournament. I had almost forgotten on the ride home.

Dad wrapped his arms around me suddenly and caught me in a suffocating hug. My breath was caught in my throat. *Dad, I just got back from Detroit. I was visiting my father.*

"I know this has been a hard few months for you, what with your slump, and this business about your birth father and everything," he whispered in my ear. "But we'll make it through together. We always do." He squeezed me hard, and I thought my ribcage might snap. He pulled back suddenly and held my shoulders in his hands. "Right?"

I could feel his hands shake—ever so slightly—on my shoulders, and I saw a deep sadness inside his eyes. It wasn't a statement, like usual. I couldn't remember the last time he really asked me something like that. *Now's your chance to tell him. Tell him.*

I turned away and picked up my bag. "You sure you want to play me?" I tried to breathe deep, but my stomach was tightening, my windpipe thick. I didn't even know if I wanted to play. It would be beautiful to prove them all wrong, that I was still the same nationally-ranked center fielder, but at the same time, I realized that how they saw me was not nearly as important to me as it had been even just a few days before.

Sonny Rollins' slippery saxophone trickled out of the speakers. Dad had it on low, always had it on low when he was working. He only played Sonny or Miles, he said, to keep him cool while he wrestled with the frustration of plays and paperwork and strategy.

Dad's brow furrowed. "Alex, of course I'm going to play you. You thought—" He cocked his head to the side and put his hand on my shoulder again.

I watched my purple Converse and imagined I had X-ray vision and could see my toes squirming inside them.

"I mean, I know . . . Like I said, it's been a difficult season for you, but that doesn't mean you're not still one of my top boys . . ."

I winced as he fumbled for words. Last year I *was* the top boy.

Dad took his hand from my shoulder and dropped it to his side. "You're going to go out there on Friday, and you're going to kick some ass. I don't want to see anything drop in that you can lay out for, I want to see you get on base five times and score four. I don't want anyone in that stadium to have any doubt that you're Terry Kirtridge's daughter."

I had heard the speech, or one like it, a million times before, and it had made me want to go out there and do everything he said, to get what he wanted, to get what I wanted. At the same time, I wondered why he couldn't just accept that I played my best.

I raised my head slowly and tried to smile. Sonny Rollins was pushing out "Autumn Leaves," my favorite track.

Dad turned away, taking my half-smile as enough, I guess, and walked back to the table. "I got so much work to do between now and then. I'm going through all of Eau Claire's games from the last three seasons, looking for holes. Called some other coaches for gossip. Seems like their slugging second baseman is actually a defensive liability. Hard slides rattle him and they've had more than a few easy double plays turn into runs. And his hitting goes to hell when he makes errors. So if we can figure out how to rattle him, we just might be able to take advantage of that . . ." He sat down, picked up a paper, and was lost in his scribbling a minute later.

I turned and started walking toward the stairs. I thought about this poor second baseman, the star hitter, the defensive liability, the one easily rattled by a hard slide. Who was he really? I was exhausted and needed to lay out my plan to reveal all to Reggie.

"Oh yeah," Dad said suddenly, breaking from his reverie. "I almost forgot—Reggie called for you."

My legs froze in place. I had told him I would call him myself—why in the world would he call the house? How did he even get the number?

"He said to call him right when you got back, that it was really important."

My stomach flipped, and I gripped my duffel strap tighter. *He got to you first*. I turned around.

Dad tapped his pen against the side of his head. "That's that kid from the Midwest Championship, right?"

I nodded.

"From East, right?"

I nodded again.

Dad shook his head. "Helluva pitcher. Could really be something some day if he trained with us."

I somehow squeaked out a "Yeah."

"I said he should come by sometime to just throw around with us, that we'd love to see him again."

Shit. "You did?"

Dad nodded. "Had a nice little chat with him, actually. He said that you and him have been hanging out a lot lately. Actually called you his girlfriend." He looked a little embarrassed, and there was no mistaking the surprise in his voice.

I put my hand over my mouth but it was too late—I hiccupped.

"I told him he should come over for dinner sometime, that we would love to meet him." Dad laughed. "We were talking about how you really don't know somebody until you know their family."

He fiddled with his pen. "I hope you don't mind, but I actually invited him and his family out with ours for a picnic sometime next weekend, after the big game's over, when we've won and everything's quiet again. I hope that's okay." He looked up at me again, hesitantly.

Fuck. Fuck. Fuck.

"I didn't tell my parents about my first girlfriend either. It's . . . something you kind of want to keep to yourself," he said. Was he trying to get me to talk more about it with him? I couldn't think of anything I was more uninterested in at that particular moment.

My face was getting redder by the minute. I wondered if he would follow me if I just bolted from the room.

"But Reggie said you two have been going out for a month now so . . . it'd be great to get to know him a little better."

I hiccupped again. Sonny Rollins had nothing more to say with his saxophone; the CD had stopped.

"Is that okay, Alex?" Dad was gnawing on his bottom lip, and he tapped his pen on the table. Each tap felt like a pin in my retina. I blinked.

"Yeah, that's cool," I said.

• • •

I met Reggie at dusk, when the heat was beginning to settle back into the ground. You could see dark clouds on the horizon, but they looked far away. "How was Milwaukee?" he asked, kicking a stone in his path. We were in Bayard Park, but we weren't running this time, just walking leisurely.

There was something in his tone—a sneer perhaps—that made me feel small. I wanted to reach out and hold his hand, I wanted to ask him to touch me, but I knew that he wouldn't. Something was different; his irritation was palpable.

"It was fine." *He's not Dad. You can tell him. You decided to tell him.* He had just gotten his hair cut again, and, studying his profile, he looked bigger than the last time I had seen him. If we faced each other, mound to plate again, I knew he would have the advantage over me. He was stronger, and I didn't like that. But I needed him.

"Yeah, your dad said you always have a great time out there with your friend and her mom, hitting all the big stores and expensive restaurants and everything," he continued. "He said you guys go out there every year."

I took a deep breath. *Tell him where you really were.* The air was heavy with rain. *He won't want you if he knows how you've lied to him in the past. He won't even believe the truth.* "Yeah, it's kind of like this girls' getaway weekend thing. Ever since we were kids, Mrs. Adams wanted us to feel like we were—"

Reggie interrupted me. "Your dad also said you've been training really hard for the game on Friday. He said that he's going to start you in center and that they'll never know what hit them when this skinny girl shows them how state titles are won." His voice was getting louder and louder, and there was no mistaking the anger that threatened to overwhelm it.

I stopped right there in the middle of the path. *I love you.* "Reggie—"

"Which got me to thinking," he said, turning around to face me. "Why am I having to hear all this from your dad and not you? Why didn't you answer my texts and calls this weekend? I called your house because I was worried something happened and then I find out you went to Milwaukee?" He took a step toward me.

I blinked. *Because I fucked up.* "I've just been—"

Reggie stopped in front of me, so his face was just inches from mine. He pursed his lips and when he released them, it took all my willpower not to cover them with my own.

"Don't!" he said. "Alex . . . How come your father seemed genuinely *interested* in meeting me and getting to know me when I called you my girlfriend? How come he didn't seem angry at all, like you said he would? Remember, a month ago, when I kept asking why you were embarrassed to let me meet your family, and you said he

164

would freak out if he knew you had a boyfriend? Remember that? Or have you just been too busy in Milwaukee or getting ready to win state to notice that just about everything you've told me about yourself is a lie?" He was yelling so loud that I had to step away.

He shook his head and then smiled wryly. "Although I guess I have no one else to blame but myself. After all, you made up that crap about your mom the first day I met you—why would anyone think that you wouldn't just keep on doing it? I'm just stupid enough to believe all of it . . ."

I was suddenly conscious that tears were streaming down my face. *This isn't happening.* "No, no," I said, wrapping my arms around his tall, angular frame. I searched my mind desperately for the words that would calm him down, the words that would make him stay. "I wasn't lying! I just . . . okay, I assumed, based on everything else I've seen my dad react to. He's so protective of me, you wouldn't believe it. And anything that could distract me or take me away from the game, he doesn't like at all, makes me try to get rid of. So I just thought . . ." I looked up at him, to see if my words were having any effect, but his expression was as cloudy as ever. *Why are you doing it again? Tell him the truth!*

Reggie pushed me away. And when he spoke, his tone was matter-of-fact; completely devoid of emotion. "You can't keep it up," he said. "It's too much to keep telling all these stories all the time. I don't even know how you can keep all of them straight." He shook his head. Then he walked right past me, back the way he had come, back toward his house.

I ran after him and grabbed his arm. "Please . . ." I said, wincing at how desperate my voice sounded in my ears. *I need you.* Why couldn't I say it? "It's got nothing to do with you. I . . ." I sighed. "I didn't want you to meet my family, okay? That's the truth. I thought you wouldn't like me anymore. Because when I'm around you, I really *feel* black, I really *am* black. But not when I'm with them, I don't know how to say it . . ." I tried to wipe away the tears, but they were coming too fast.

He shook my hand off his arm and looked at me like I was the stone he had kicked only minutes before—misshapen and dirty. Then he walked toward me one last time and touched my hair; my straightened, beautiful hair, which I had washed, blown dry and set specially for our meeting. "I don't care how you talk or do your hair or walk," he said softly. "I care that you lie."

The park was desolate except for two kids aimlessly kicking a ball around.

He turned, and started walking.

"Just . . . wait," I said, reaching for him. "Reggie, don't."

He kept walking.

"Reggie!" I yelled. "Reggie!"

But no matter how many times I called to him, he would not turn around.

CHAPTER TWENTY-EIGHT

Kit shook her head. "Fuck," she said. Even I had to admit that hanging out with me more was beginning to negatively affect her formerly very clean vocabulary.

I shifted my weight in a plush leather chair in my room and chewed on a chocolate bar. We could hear Mom in the kitchen downstairs, clanging pots and pans, searching for something to make for dinner.

Kit pushed a strand of her thin blonde hair behind an ear. "Call him in a week and see how it goes," she said. "He'll have cooled down by then."

I picked at a callus on the side of my big toe. *You could have loved him, but you messed it up.*

"He just thinks you dissed him," she said, grabbing a gummy worm from the bag.

I sighed. "I *did* diss him."

"Okay, but does he even have a clue about all the stuff that's going on with you right now? I mean sure, you haven't handled it the best, but how would he be with you if he had just met his real father?"

I lifted my index finger. "Biological father," I said.

Kit waved her hand. "Whatever."

I rolled my eyes. She really didn't get that Keith wasn't any more my father than Dad was. It wasn't a question of blood or race or lineage or upbringing. It was a question, I was beginning to see, of what I wanted.

"The point is that Reggie should get that you're not exactly at the top of your game, having just visited Keith and his family in Detroit," Kit said. "I mean, didn't he flip out when you told him about sitting down at the dinner table with them, meeting your half-sister and debating the merits of religion with his wife? Didn't he get a little less angry when you told him about all those letters that Keith wrote you?"

I shrugged. I ripped off a layer of dead skin from my toe.

"Alex," Kit said, leaning in closer. "You did tell him about the letters, right?"

I dug into my toe deeper, even though all of the dead skin was gone. I picked at the delicate, pink skin around the eviscerated callus, and ripped off a small patch. Blood oozed up from underneath. *I need you.*

"Well, fuck," said Kit. She threw up her hands. "Then I guess you didn't tell him about Detroit either."

I pressed down on my toe as hard as I could. *Pressure stops the bleeding.*

"I have to say that I'm seeing his side of it a little more than yours at this particular moment in time, even though you are my only sister, and I take your side in all things by default."

I shivered, remembering his right hand moving down the small of my back. His teeth on my earlobe. *Never again.*

"What about Keith?" Kit asked, leaning her head against the wall. Her skin looked so white in that moment against the brightness of the paint.

"What about him?" I asked.

"When are you going to see him again? Are you going to talk to him again?"

I was pressing my toe so hard that I couldn't even feel it anymore. *I would like to meet you someday. I am your father. There was a lot of things that could have been better between your mother and I. I would have liked the chance to know you.*

"I don't know," I said. *The most important thing is that a child be raised under the eyes of God. No matter what color the family.* "It's . . . complicated."

Kit nodded. I looked into her light gray eyes, and for the first time in over a year, I saw tears in their depths. She never cried—even in front of me. "Yeah," she said.

I tried to smile. "But I'd like to visit him—them—again."

CHAPTER
TWENTY-NINE

On the day of the state tournament quarterfinal, we got to the field four hours before the game. It was at Bowman Field on UW, which boasted a seating capacity of 4,500 and consistently the freshest cut grass in the conference. We had watched the Badgers lose to Purdue here two years ago during the Big Ten championship, and now here we were, getting ready to play for a championship in front of thousands of spectators.

"I want you to pay extra attention to your plyometrics today," Dad said, the brim of his cap obscuring his eyes. "I don't want to see any dead arms, and I don't want to see anyone standing on the ground for longer than a second after each jump."

Logan looked down and rolled his eyes. He was a reliever and wouldn't pitch for a couple hours if at all, yet Dad always made him do the full warm-up with us. He said it fostered a sense of equal responsibility among team members.

"What, you think your quads and calves are all warmed up already?" Dad asked Logan, walking toward him slowly.

I shook my head. Logan had been playing with Dad for almost as long as Jason and I had, yet he had somehow managed not to learn that Dad saw *everything*.

"You think your teammates would do better if you weren't here, warming up with them?" Dad asked him, his face barely an inch away, his eyes flashing with anger.

Logan bit his lip. I was sure there were about a million places he would rather be right at that moment. "No, Coach Kirtridge," he said. "I know what it takes to be a member of the team."

It was always better if you used Dad's language when you found yourself in a scrape.

Logan looked Dad in the eyes. "I'm ready to lead the box jump." That was the first drill.

Dad adjusted his cap. "Good," he said. He surveyed the field, watching all of us sprawled out on the grass at strange angles, stretching our backs and arms and calves. "And all of you better get ready, too," he said, gesturing toward us. "Because this is a game where everybody's going to have to step up and play harder and smarter and just plain *better* than they ever have before."

We understood we should stop stretching and give him our full attention. I pulled my right leg from my chest, and then set it on the grass.

"Eau Claire isn't just any team," Dad said, walking around our small circle of fifteen. "They have been a top-ranked team in the nation for the past five seasons running. Last season, they scored more runs than any team in the history of Wisconsin high school baseball."

I sniffed and kicked at a patch of grass. *You're going to go out there on Friday, and you're going to kick some ass.*

"Eau Claire has a winning tradition," Dad continued, enunciating each word carefully. "They think they're going to just knock us over with their trophy case."

Dad took several more steps and stopped in front of me. "They can talk like that all they want, and they can spend the rest of the year polishing their old trophies for all I care."

It was a hot day—around 95 degrees. My eyes were smarting, even through my sunglasses. Drops of sweat were crawling down my forehead.

Dad turned to his left and faced me. "And why is that, Alex?"

I don't want to see you let anything drop in that you can lay out for, I want to see you get on base five times and score four. I wiped my forehead with the back of my hand, but I only succeeded in knocking some of the sweat into my eyes. They stung, and I winced. "Because . . ." I said, racking my brain for the sentence that he wanted. "Because it shows they're not focused." I tried to make it sound as much like a definitive statement as possible, but it came out sounding more like a question.

Dad scratched the back of his ear. On the other side of the field, Eau Claire was just walking into their dugout, dropping their gear on the bench. A slight wind blew over us, ruffling our jerseys, and making the hair on my neck stand up. "No," he said. "Because it shows they have a lack of respect. Their tradition isn't swinging a bat today. Their old titles won't make them run just a little harder. Only respect will."

Across from me, Jason crossed his arms and nodded.

"And without respect," he said, looking deep into my eyes, "you have nothing."

I nodded. It was his automatic response, like scratching a mosquito bite or pulling your hand away from fire, but it still irritated me. Why was 90 percent of what came out of his mouth scripted? I sighed; I was just here to play a game.

Logan was staring blankly out into space. Dad walked over to him and took his chin in his hand. "You—we—have nothing," he said, startling Logan out of his reverie. "Our team has gotten so far because you respect me enough to listen to what I have to teach you and because you respect yourselves enough to do the work it takes to learn and then apply that learning in order to win games."

I kicked at the patch of grass harder, sending a few clumps of dirt flying.

Dad crossed his arms. "That's really all it takes," he said. "But it's a lot if you don't have it in here." He tapped his head. "All that stuff I told you guys all these years about the game all being psychology, that wasn't just a bunch of horseshit."

Norm guffawed and everyone glared at him.

Dad continued his walk around our circle, trying to catch each of us with his eyes. "Everything I do, everything I say, has a reason," Dad said.

Across from me, Jason was staring at Dad like he was Jesus Christ himself.

"All the weight I make you lift, all the running, all the drills, are nothing compared to the mental fortitude it takes to win a major championship. And these jokers," he gestured toward Eau Claire with his head, "have forgotten that." Dad smiled. "They've gotten way too comfortable with the idea of winning to realize that it's just that—an idea—until you decide to do the work to make it happen in the world."

Some of my teammates shook their heads. When Dad waxed philosophical like this before big games, it invariably confused a third of our team. But he continued, undaunted. "You have to get yourself in a zone where *no one* and *nothing* can come in and distract you from your one, singular goal of making that catch, turning that double play, beating the tag till you think your damn lungs will explode—understand?"

A few of us nodded. Dad's brow furrowed. "I asked if you understood," he said.

"Yes," a bunch of us murmured.

My stomach was churning with all this talking, my windpipe beginning to constrict. *When will he just let us be? We know how to play—he taught us.*

"Let them think we're scared of their tradition. The more energy they put into that idea, the more energy we put into our fielding, and all the plays we've been going over and over for months now." He looked at Jason and then at me. "Even years."

Eau Claire were running out of their dugout and jogging en masse around the field. It wouldn't be long now before the game started. It wouldn't be long now before all the trust that Dad ever had in me would be put to the test. He could have played Kyle in center easily—Kyle had been working incredibly hard the past few weeks, trying to show Dad that he had no choice but to play him in one of the most important games of his coaching life, that he had to let go of his daughter and decide that what he wanted more was to win, and that Kyle could make this decision as clear, and as painless, as possible. But Dad wasn't falling for it. If there was one principle that guided him, it was that anything was possible. No barrier was intractable if you worked hard enough. And I had worked, and I was his daughter.

"The only end to this game is victory," he told us, stepping outside our circle. "That's the only possibility I want in your mind for the next six hours." He pulled his stopwatch out of his pocket and clicked its knob with his index finger. "Logan," he said. "You're the first one in the box. Let's go."

We all lined up behind Logan, two feet away from the box, as he squatted down and prepared to jump.

• • •

Our pitching was dominant for the first few innings, so I saw no action in center. And I was hitting eighth, so our three-run first inning happened without my bat. In other words, three innings of standing alone in center were all I needed for Dad's plan to become clear. In truth, he was the one lacking in respect for his opponent. He was confident that he had solved Eau Claire's lineup. He was confident that through sheer force of his will and maniacal preparation, we would win this game even with a liability at center. And even I could see that he saw this as the act of a loving father.

• • •

By the sixth inning, Eau Claire had gotten one run off of us, and held us to the three runs we had managed in the first.

"I want to see some passion out there," Dad yelled at us in the dugout. "You all are acting like you're just waiting to see how the game turns out. Cal, you almost let their catcher reach on a weak ground ball; a championship shortstop doesn't make half-assed plays like that. Darren, you made that catch in the second inning look a lot harder than it should have been. This isn't Little League, ladies."

I winced, retying my spikes, which never seemed to be tight enough.

"No, this is the fucking *championship*," Dad said. He pointed to the field. "And I coach a team of champions. Now get out there and start acting like one!"

Yes, he wanted me in this game for me, but I also saw that it was for him, too. Terry Kirtridge's children were ballplayers, starters, and champions. This fact was as important to who he was as to who Jason and I were. Probably more.

I shoved my mitt under my arm and jogged out to my spot in center field, right. *If we can hold them here, there's only one more inning to go.* I put my hand in the glove and let my fingers find the tunnels they had carved out in the leather. I punched the mitt's palm with my right hand, noticing that its color was not so different from the mitt's. *Just a few shades lighter.* I peered toward the plate. The next guy up, their on-base guy, was short and skinny, but I could see he was also muscular.

Logan went into the windup, taking a short step behind him. Then as he pivoted his stride foot, lifting his knee to his chest, he brought his hands down between his belt and chest. He cocked his throwing arm back as far as it would go, and shifting his weight forward, he brought his throwing arm over the top and released. The skinny guy stayed crouched, tapped his toe on the dirt to get his timing, and strode toward the ball, fighting off the inside pitch with the handle of his bat. The ball blooped over third, slapping down just inside the outfield grass.

"Damn," I said, running toward Darren, our left fielder, to back him up. I looked toward Dad in the dugout. Sure enough, his arms were crossed, and he was pacing. I shook my head. Then I peered into the bleachers, trying to find Mom and Kit. Grandma Kirtridge and Aunt Gwen had even driven down from Saint Paul to see the game, but I couldn't spot them either.

On the mound, Logan took off his hat and wiped his brow. His blond hair was curly and slightly unruly, spilling out in all directions. I remembered when we were nine and his mom had cut it in the shape of a bowl and we all teased him. I stifled a laugh. Watching him flex his hands and kick at the dirt on the mound, I saw that he was the same person I knew seven years ago—he had just gotten bigger and allowed Dad to nurture the side of him that was an amazing pitcher so that it grew and grew and almost eclipsed every other part of him. But I knew that Logan loved to draw as much as he loved pitching. He had a sketchbook he had shown me on a few road trips, and the drawings were actually quite good.

The next hitter came to the plate. He looked like he was Latino. He crossed himself. I remembered the scouting report on him then—Hector Sanchez. Shortstop. Led the league in doubles and triples. Dad had given the infielders a shift just for him. I glanced toward Jason to see if he was ready, if he knew who we were dealing with, and I could see from the forward torque of his upper body that he knew, that he would run at the blink of an eye. Which would be exactly what Dad expected, demanded.

Logan went into the stretch, and the pitch was in Jerry's glove before I could see it. The umpire called a strike, and I exhaled. When Logan was on, most hitters had no idea what was happening—their whole at bat was over before they knew it. He worked fast and threw hard. *Half the battle is showing the hitter who's in charge—him or the pitcher. Once you have that decided, the rest is like a big boulder rolling down a hill. It's all just gravity and momentum, and who can stop them?* How many times had I heard Dad say that?

176

Hector stepped into the batter's box once again, not appearing flummoxed at all. He waved his bat around in back of him, like a bee circling something it wanted to sting. My attention had flagged for only a second, but it was enough. When I focused again, Logan was already finishing up his follow-through, and Hector was swinging, this time at a high fastball. I felt my breath catch in my windpipe, and I crouched down, getting ready.

But all Hector got was air. His bat swung around, and when he blinked again, the ball was safely in Jerry's glove, untouched. I grinned; apparently, Hector was not all his scouting report said he was.

On the mound, Logan took off his hat again and wiped his brow. The sun felt relentless on my back, even though I knew that we had only been out on the field for about ten minutes for that inning. I wanted water and somewhere to lie down and sleep. It was exhausting out here—the dull roar of the crowd deafened your ears if you didn't know how to tune it out. Seven innings seemed too long, somehow, to stand it. Logan put his hat back on and licked his lips. *Come on Log, you got it. I know you do.* He stretched his arms above his head, brought his hands down, and pushed off from the pitching rubber. Hector tensed up as the pitch came at him, brought his bat around a little quicker and a little higher than he had before, and connected this time. The ball went flying toward third, and the runner took off from first, already halfway there when Jason dove into the dirt, and the ball bounced off the edge of his mitt and bounced into short left field. Hector bolted for first and made it there easily, right as Darren picked up the ball in short left. The short, skinny guy, who also happened to be fast, slid into third a moment later, and there we were, the bottom of the sixth, no outs and the go-ahead run at the plate. I sighed.

Dad took a time-out and walked onto the mound to consult with Logan. Even though we were playing at home, Eau Claire had somehow managed to pack the stands with their fans. I suddenly noticed them, standing and shouting.

I pounded my mitt and glanced into our bullpen. Bill was warming up. Dad had probably had him warming up since the beginning of the inning, just to be on the safe side. Dad usually wasn't one to panic and pull a pitcher early. *A winner fights through the jam*, he'd said countless times. But it was clear this game was different.

On the mound, Dad was patting Logan's back and nodding. Logan looked both sad and resigned as he handed Dad the ball and jogged toward the dugout.

Bill emerged from the bullpen as Logan walked to the dugout. I zoned out for Bill's warmup tosses, and before I knew it, the ump yelled, "Play ball." I looked around, startled, making sure I was in position relative to everyone else. We were all standing left of center, so I shifted myself a bit.

Eau Claire's next hitter was a big righty pull hitter, which was why we all were shaded left. He had a wide stance, and looked to me like he was crowding the plate. But I knew Bill would cure him of that affliction soon enough, throwing him something that would come close enough to knock him on his ass. Bill stood sideways on the mound, peering at Jerry for what felt like the longest moment of my life, holding the ball in his right index and middle fingers. Jerry gave him a few signs, and Bill shook his head. I crouched down, conscious of the sweat rolling down my chest, in between my breasts. The heat and my thirst were brutal and my vision flashed double for a second. Jerry gave Bill another sign and this time, Bill nodded. He shifted the ball in his hand behind him a bit, dragged his arm and glove over his head, and then reached back behind him. Bill's motion was like a huge wave, and his follow-through always seemed like it would knock him over. He rattled a lot of batters the first time they faced him.

This hitter didn't blink, though. He didn't jump at the ball. He took his time and waited for the ball to come to him. It was the perfect pitch to hit, right down the middle, and he hit it hard and deliberately, straight to center field, straight to me. After almost two hours, I was finally part of the game. As the ball tunneled through the air and sped further and further back, I could see that this was a play Terry Kirtridge's daughter had made a million times before, one which would get the first out of the inning, and maybe the second if the runner on third was foolish enough to test her arm.

I ran toward where I knew the ball would drop, just a few steps to my right. If I just held out Terry Kirtridge's daughter's glove, the ball would fall right into it and that would be that. As it sped toward me, I saw Dad congratulating his daughter on her heads-up play, I saw him and Jason slapping backs and exchanging hugs, I saw every game Terry Kirtridge's daughter had ever played in her life—wet, rainy, sunny, clear, endlessly long, brilliantly short—and I saw them blur into each other until they were all the same in their perfection and disappointment. And then, I saw myself step away from the ball. It landed inches from where I stood and fell on the grass. I watched its red stitching roll over, roll over, roll over, and then finally stop.

CHAPTER THIRTY

Fall was always my favorite season. The air cooler, crisper, the sun dimmer through the dying leaves. And yet, even through these smaller endings, everything in my world always started back up again with a burst of energy: School. Baseball. Friendships. The thrill of the new was so liberating every year, but this year especially. This year I was a senior. And this year I would not be playing baseball.

Even though we lost the quarterfinals and therefore, the tournament, it was not my fault. Yes, I intentionally missed the catch. Yes, Dad was possibly more pissed about this than I have ever seen him. He benched me for the rest of the game, and I still watched them fumble everything to a loss. They even got ahead for half an inning, but then buckled in the seventh after our pitcher handed their third baseman a triple with a man on base. Maybe they were unfocused, or maybe they didn't want it bad enough. Maybe Eau Claire just wanted it more. But they lost. Sitting there on the bench, what I realized was that I didn't even care.

Afterward, over a long and painful father-daughter lunch at Elle's, Dad told me that he knew I was under a lot of pressure, and that he understood everything. He said it was because of Keith's letters they had kept from me; he said that it was the stress of trying to negotiate my first romantic relationship; he said I had done it because I was angry about my body changing. But these were not reasons to quit playing ball. Not really. I told him he was right, and that the reason I was quitting was that I just didn't want to do it anymore. Of course he didn't listen. Of course he argued—he's my dad. But he was gradually coming to accept it, mostly because he didn't have a choice. It was my decision, after all.

To watch a leaf fall, to feel it glide all the way down, that was what I wanted this season. Not for the landing but just for the push and pull of the current, the unexpected flip. The detour that turned out to be the destination. I was ready for organic chemistry, couldn't wait for AP English, and to let my arm really rest while holding *Crime and Punishment*. High school would be over before I knew it and before I left, I wanted to suck it dry of everything I could get. Perhaps I would do it alone, perhaps with a few intimate others like Kit, but I would no longer feel the need to eschew what had brought me into being, and what I still could neither explain nor answer for. I would not apologize for the shame I felt in my skin. At the same time, I recognized it and tried to see its value. I would no longer assume that my safest starting place in all things was my parents or my family, but the dream that some softer other space existed to hold me—all of my different, conflicting parts—was now dead, as well. What had taken hold instead was a longing for some kind of ever-shifting community, which I would have to carry with me wherever I went because there was no way it could ever exist all in one place. I was mixed. I was black. I was adopted by white people and loved by them. And I loved them back, even though they didn't know so much of me, and even though this hurt me. I was a child of my birth father, but maybe not his daughter. And once upon a time, I had played ball. And once upon a time I had let it go. All these pieces had cracked me open and brought me to this place of danger and possibility.

I was ready.

ACKNOWLEDGMENTS

So many people and communities have supported the evolution of this project, and I am deeply indebted to each and every one of them.

A huge, larger-than-life thanks to my editor extraordinaire, Andrew Karre, whose hard work, keen insights, and affinity for this story were invaluable to its development. Seldom have I worked with a sharper mind.

Thanks to Betty Tisel and Swati Avasthi, who put me in touch with Andrew Karre, and to Carolrhoda Lab and Lerner Publishing Group, for all the resources you marshaled to bring this book into being.

Thank you to all my readers, whose candor and encouragement kept me going even when I was sure all the narrative threads would not come together: Karen Hausdoerffer, Patrice Johnson, Christopher Cross, Kenna Cottman, Tayari Jones, Dana Johnson, Tony Ardizzone, Sarah Dahlen, Bobbi Chase Wilding, Sara Buckwitz, Elaine Kim, Kurtis Scaletta, Kathleen DeVore, Beverly Cottman, Mary Lou Iroegbu, Kathy Solomon, and Evelyn Fazio, the first commercial editor who really "got" the story, believed in its potential, and gave me key suggestions for revision; the students and faculty of the Indiana University MFA fiction program who read and critiqued very early and very rough drafts; (then) teens Lucie Barton, Srija Sen Chatterjea, and Abdishe Dorose, whose feedback and support were essential to me during a time when I was sure that this story had no real audience; and the Bush Foundation, who gave me the time, space, and funding to dig deeper.

Thank you, Jae Ran Kim, for your expertise in all things child-welfare related.

Thanks to Kevin Haebeom Vollmers and Adam Chau of CQT Publishing and Land of a Gazillion Adoptees, for first taking a chance on this manuscript.

Thanks to my husband, Ballah Corvah, son, Boisey Corvah, and daughter, Marwein Corvah, for giving me the space and inspiration to write.

Thank you, Jim and Sue Gibney, for always believing I would get it done.

And last, but hardly least, thank you, global transracial adoptee community, for the revelation that this story is not mine, but ours.

See No Color by Shannon Gibney
READING GROUP GUIDE

||||||||||||||||||||||||||||||||||||||||||||||||||||||||||||||||||||||||||||||||||||||||||||

1. Alex has always known that she was adopted. Why have her parents never spoken of the details of her adoption? Define "malady." What makes Alex wonder if she has a malady that her parents haven't revealed to her? At what point does she discover what that malady is? How does this make Alex feel like a "product"?

2. Explain the term "transracial adoptee." Debate whether this term makes Alex feel any different about being a biracial child adopted by white parents. Discuss Alex's experience in the beauty salon. What does this reveal about acceptance and identity?

3. Discuss Alex's relationship with Kit, her younger sister. How does their relationship change when Kit begins probing into the circumstances of Alex's adoption? Debate whether Kit is really considering Alex's feelings when she questions Alex's ethnicity. Alex's mom says, "We are all one in this family, okay? We don't even see color." (p. 27) Cite incidents in the novel that support the idea that her mom's statement is both true and false.

4. Kit grows bolder and brasher throughout the novel. Alex tells her sister, "I just don't understand why you felt the need to get involved in something that doesn't concern you." (p. 54) Why does Kit continue to meddle in the facts surrounding Alex's adoption? Explain why Kit is determined to find out what it feels like to be biracial in a white family. Alex's dad senses that Kit is getting to Alex. He says, "I just wish there were things I knew how to talk about with you." (p. 57) When are Alex's parents planning to share details of her adoption with her? Debate whether it's her parents or Alex who can't handle the truth?

5. Discuss what Kit means when she says to Alex, "You're uncomfortable being uncomfortable." (p. 141) Cite scenes in the novel when Alex appears the most "uncomfortable." How does Kit contribute to this "discomfort"? Explain Alex's "discomfort" with Reggie, her boyfriend. What is Kit referencing when she says, "I'm comfortable being uncomfortable. Maybe that's the difference."? (p. 141)

6. Alex's mother is angry when she finds that Alex has read the folder marked "Alex's Adoption." Why does she refer to Alex's biological father as "that man"? Jason is Alex's younger brother. How does he react to Alex reading the folder? Why does Alex believe that she and Jason will never be as close as they had been in the past?

7. Alex calls her biological father and visits him in Detroit. What did she expect from the reunion? What does she find? Alex calls Reggie to tell him about meeting her biological father. Explain Reggie's reaction to her. Discuss what Alex means when she says, "I was a child of my birth father, but maybe not his daughter." (pp. 181–82) How does this statement suggest that she understands the real meaning of family?

8. Alex is a star player on her father's baseball team at West High. Explain how the following statement reveals what Alex's father values the most: "When you don't play your best, you don't just hurt yourself. You hurt me." (p. 4) How does her father react when Alex intentionally misses a catch in the quarterfinals? At the end of the novel, she mentions that she has been brought to a "place of danger and possibility." (p. 182) What is the danger? What is the possibility?

9. Explain the image on the cover of the book. What is the symbolism of the baseball? How does it reveal Alex's journey?

About the Author

Shannon Gibney is an award-winning author of books of all kinds—from novels to anthologies to essays to picture books. She writes for adults, children, and everyone in between. Shannon's books and writings have received many awards, and are taught in schools and communities around the country. She is a professor of English at Minneapolis College, where for more than twelve years she has worked with refugees, ex-offenders, international and in-country immigrants, indigenous and communities of color, and students from all walks of life to tell their stories and achieve their academic and professional goals.

Shannon identifies as a transracial adoptee, and was adopted by white parents in Ann Arbor, Michigan, in 1975. She writes and speaks extensively about transracial adoption in her creative and scholarly work, and of the intersection of race, gender, class, family, power, and identity. This experience has informed all her work with and about historically and newly marginalized communities.

Reading Group Guide prepared by Pat Scales, retired school librarian and independent consultant, Greenville, South Carolina.